**Fremdsprachentexte**

# English Love Stories

Herausgegeben von



Philipp Reclam jun. Stuttgart

Universal-Bibliothek Nr. 9047

Copyright-Vermerke für die Texte siehe Seite 165 f.
Gesamtherstellung: Reclam, Ditzingen. Printed in Germany 2002
RECLAM und UNIVERSAL-BIBLIOTHEK sind eingetragene Marken der Philipp Reclam jun. GmbH & Co., Stuttgart
ISBN 3-15-009047-4

www.reclam.de

# Inhalt

# Vorwort

*Love Stories* – das klingt, zumal für das deutsche Ohr, ein bißchen verdächtig. Vorstellungen von schmelzender Süße und rassiger Leidenschaft stellen sich ein, von denen andere literarische Gattungen, die sich mit demselben Thema befassen, das Liebesgedicht beispielsweise, weitgehend unbelastet sind. Daß das so ist, beruht sicher nicht nur auf der Existenz eines breiten Sektors der Trivialliteratur, der Liebe in Form von Kitsch erfolgreich vermarktet. Die Gattung der Kurzgeschichte selbst mit ihren eigenen Erfordernissen steht in einem gewissen Spannungsverhältnis zum Thema »Liebe«, dessen Nichtbeachtung von negativer Konsequenz für die literarische Qualität sein kann und die Nähe zum Kitsch möglicherweise provoziert. Die Form der Kurzgeschichte, die das dargestellte Geschehen in konzentrierter und dramatischer Weise zur Krise treibt, hat eine deutliche Affinität zu menschlicher Leidenschaft, doch nur eine geringe zum Glück, kaum eine zum Happy-End. Liebe als Thema der Kurzgeschichte erscheint daher häufig gebunden an Umbruchsituationen, die die psychologischen und gesellschaftlichen Bedingtheiten menschlicher Beziehungen erhellen. Es sind viel eher die Brüche und Defizite im Zusammenleben, die emotionale Unfähigkeit des einzelnen, der Kampf der Geschlechter und das Scheitern von Illusionen als die Erfüllung und Idealisierung von Liebe, die in der Kurzgeschichte ihr Medium finden. So ist der Begriff »Beziehungsgeschichten«, der in letzter Zeit manchmal dem der »Liebesgeschichten«

vorgezogen wird, nicht nur als terminologische Anpassung an einen gesellschaftlichen Trend zu sehen, sondern durchaus als ein Hinweis auf die Besonderheiten und die inhaltliche Vielfalt des Genres. Andererseits ergibt sich eben aus dieser Vielfalt eine perspektivenreiche Annäherung an das Phänomen »Liebe«. Gerade die Krisen und Konflikte loten die Bedingungen und Möglichkeiten und häufig die Unmöglichkeit eines Gefühls aus, das dennoch als Wunsch oder Ziel oder auch nur als Ahnung präsent ist.

Die vorliegende Anthologie möchte daher Liebesgeschichten vorstellen, die diesem Begriff in seinem weiter gefaßten Sinn gerecht werden und trotz der erforderlichen Beschränkung auf neun Geschichten ein Spektrum an Akzenten erkennen lassen, die nicht nur die Vielfalt des Themas, sondern auch zeitbedingte Unterschiede innerhalb des 20. Jahrhunderts sichtbar machen. Die chronologische Anordnung soll – mit einer Geschichte aus fast jedem Jahrzehnt – eine Entwicklung nachzeichnen, wobei sich aber auch deutliche Beziehungen unabhängig von der Chronologie ergeben.

Eine Motivverwandtschaft verbindet beispielsweise D. H. Lawrences »Second Best« und Ian McEwans »First Love, Last Rites«. Die Tötung eines Tieres – eines Maulwurfs, einer Ratte – wird zum Symbol der zwischenmenschlichen Beziehung. Der blind tastende Maulwurf verkörpert blinde, instinkthafte Leidenschaft; mit seiner Tötung vollzieht Frances ihre Unterwerfung unter ihre sexuellen Bedürfnisse, aber auch eine Anerkennung derselben, die sie den Zweitbesten wählen läßt, nachdem ihre eher gesellschaftlich ambitionierte erste Liebe enttäuscht wurde. Die Tötung der

Ratte dagegen, deren geborstener Körper ungeborene Junge freigibt, läßt das junge Paar im Sinne einer Initiation die kindliche Unbekümmertheit ihrer bisher gelebten Sexualität aufgeben und die Verantwortung des Erwachsenenlebens begreifen. Die ältere Geschichte insistiert auf der Aufdeckung unterschwelliger triebgeleiteter Motivationen der scheinbar konventionellen Partnerwahl, die neuere stattet ihre jugendlichen Protagonisten mit dem aufgeklärten Bewußtsein der siebziger Jahre aus, das mit dem Wissen über biochemische Fakten Sexualität rationalisiert hat und erst zu einem Erkennen der Defizite dieser Sichtweise und einer Synthese von Wissen und Handeln heranreifen muß.

Während die Symbolik bei Lawrence zum Ausdruck des Erotischen eingesetzt wird, verwendet Katherine Mansfield sie zur sinnfälligen Darstellung wechselnder Gefühlszustände. Weniger subtil vielleicht als in manchen ihrer anderen Geschichten, aber sehr effektvoll werden Gesten, Farben, Licht, Geräusche und Musik zum Abbild der Seele der Musiklehrerin. Die scheinbare Naivität der Darstellung verliert jedoch ihre harmlose Leichtigkeit, indem sie mit Untertönen, die auf die Abhängigkeit in der Beziehung und die dieser entsprechenden Willkür in der Behandlung der Schülerinnen verweisen, durchsetzt wird. Beide, Lawrence wie Mansfield, geben der modernen Kurzgeschichte und zumal der Liebesgeschichte am Anfang des Jahrhunderts durch ihre Gestaltungsweisen des Psychologischen wesentliche Impulse.

Eine Beziehung thematischer Art, wenn auch in gegensätzlicher Ausprägung verbindet Frank O'Connors

»Judas« und Doris Lessings »Flight«. Liebe erscheint hier als enge Bindung, die den Freiraum des einzelnen eingrenzt und seine Entwicklung behindert. So ist bei Lessing die Liebe des Großvaters zu seiner Enkelin das eigentliche Thema – die Liebe des jungen Paares wird demgegenüber als ein Stadium des natürlichen Lebenskreislaufs betrachtet. Die Notwendigkeit des Loslassens und das Akzeptieren eben dieses Lebenskreislaufs führen bei Lessing im Bild der fliegenden Taube zu Befreiung und Stolz angesichts des Sieges über sich selbst, bei O'Connor jedoch endet die zunächst humoristisch anmutende Beschreibung der Beziehungsprobleme des jugendlichen Ich-Erzählers in umklammernder, eifersüchtiger Mutterliebe, die, wie im Rückblick deutlich wird, ein selbstbestimmtes Leben und Lieben des Sohnes im Keim erstickt. Die Radikalität der Frustration eigener Wünsche durch die überwältigende Macht des verinnerlichten moralischen Zwanges erinnert an O'Connors irischen Landsmann James Joyce, der in »Eveline« eine ähnliche Abhängigkeit gestaltete. Die jüngste Geschichte dieser Anthologie, Anne Enrights »Seascape«, stellt sich in diese Tradition irischer Erzähler, indem sie ein modernes Liebespaar in Auseinandersetzung mit einer konservativen körperfeindlichen Moral zeigt, die – obschon überwunden geglaubt – Unfreiheit schafft, die in subtiler Form die Kommunikation der beiden und damit eine vertrauensvolle Partnerschaft behindert. Radikaler noch zeigt Fay Weldon in »The School Run«, wie eine enttabuisierte Sexualität keine Befreiung, sondern neue Zwänge schafft, so daß die vordergründig konventionell erscheinende Rückkehr der Frau zu Mann und Familie den eigentlichen

Akt der Emanzipation und Selbstbestimmung darstellt. Wie weit hier die Kurzgeschichte zum Spiegel einer gesellschaftlichen Entwicklung und eines veränderten Bewußtseins der Rolle der Frau wird, macht ein Vergleich mit der fünfzig Jahre älteren Geschichte »The Needlecase« von Elizabeth Bowen deutlich. Dort sind gesellschaftliche Konventionen und gesellschaftlicher Ehrgeiz Maßstäbe und Fesseln individuellen Handelns, die das gefallene Mädchen ebenso um ihr Lebensglück bringen wie den Sohn aus verarmtem Herrschaftshaus, wobei sich erstere ihren Stolz, letzterer die innere Leere eines an materiellen Werten orientierten Lebens bewahrt. Bei Weldon gibt es kein gefallenes Mädchen mehr, sondern eine Frau, die selbst die Initiative ihrer sexuellen Bedürfnisse ergreift und die Spießigkeit gesellschaftlicher Normen verachtet, um festzustellen, daß sie in ihrer vermeintlichen Freiheit nur um so tiefer in die Abhängigkeit von männlichem Dominanzgebaren gerät, und letztlich erkennt, daß dem einzelnen mit der Befreiung von überkommenen Konventionen auch die Verantwortung für die Wertmaßstäbe und den Sinn der eigenen Lebensgestaltung aufgegeben ist. An letzterem Punkt genau scheitert der Protagonist von Penelope Livelys »The Art of Biography«, dessen Beschäftigung mit einem anderen Leben und einer anderen Liebe, die er biographisch aufzuarbeiten hat, zum Ersatzleben wird, das die eigene Liebesunfähigkeit offenkundig macht.

Liebe als Thema von Literatur, das machen die neun Geschichten deutlich, ist immer auch Erkundung und Darstellung von Lebensganzheit. In seiner Liebe und Leidenschaft werden Lebensgestaltung, Lebensphilosophie, Sinnfindung oder gescheitertes, unmündiges, fremdbestimmtes Leben des Protagonisten wie in einem Brennpunkt deutlich; sein Ich steht im Mittelpunkt des Erzählens. Die Beziehung zum Partner ist vor allem insofern interessant, als sie dieses Ich erkennbar macht. So kann im Extremfall der geliebte Mensch wie bei Mansfield oder Lively so weit aus der Geschichte verschwinden, daß er gar nicht mehr physisch auf dem Schauplatz vorhanden ist. Andererseits wird der Schauplatz selbst, die natürliche oder künstliche Umgebung, in vielfältiger Weise zum Spiegel innerer Prozesse, die die Liebe wie die Lebensentwicklung an einem entscheidenden Wendepunkt zeigen. So gesehen können gerade Liebesgeschichten als exemplarisch für die Gattung der Kurzgeschichte gelten.

*Eva-Maria König*

D. H. Lawrence

# Second Best

"Oh, I'm tired!" Frances exclaimed petulantly, and in the same instant she dropped down on the turf, near the hedge-bottom. Anne stood a moment surprised, then, accustomed to the vagaries of her beloved Frances, said:

"Well, and aren't you always likely to be tired, after travelling that blessed long way from Liverpool yesterday?" and she plumped down beside her sister. Anne was a wise young body of fourteen, very buxom, brimming with common sense. Frances was much older, about twenty-three, and whimsical, spasmodic. She was the beauty and the clever child of the family. She plucked the goose-grass buttons from her dress in a nervous, desperate fashion. Her beautiful profile, looped above

3 **petulantly** (adv.): gereizt, launisch.
4 **turf:** Rasen.
6 **vagary:** Laune, Extravaganz.
9 **blessed** (coll.): verwünscht, verflucht.
10 **to plump down:** sich fallen lassen.
11 **body:** Person.
**buxom:** drall, robust; munter.
11 f. **to brim:** bis zum Rand voll sein, überquellen.
12 **common sense:** gesunder Menschenverstand.
13 **whimsical:** launenhaft, verquer.
**spasmodic:** unausgeglichen, sprunghaft, unstet.
15 **goose-grass button:** Labkrautknospe, -blüte.
16 **to loop:** umschlingen.

with black hair, warm with the dusky-and-scarlet complexion of a pear, was calm as a mask, her thin brown hand plucked nervously.

"It's not the journey," she said, objecting to Anne's obtuseness. Anne looked inquiringly at her darling. The young girl, in her self-confident, practical way, proceeded to reckon up this whimsical creature. But suddenly she found herself full in the eyes of Frances; felt two dark, hectic eyes flaring challenge at her, and she shrank away. Frances was peculiar for these great, exposed looks, which disconcerted people by their violence and their suddenness.

"What's a matter, poor old duck?" asked Anne, as she folded the slight, wilful form of her sister in her arms. Frances laughed shakily, and nestled down for comfort on the budding breasts of the strong girl.

"Oh, I'm only a bit tired," she murmured, on the point of tears.

1 **dusky-and-scarlet:** dunkelbraun und -rot.
2 **mask:** Maske.
4 f. **obtuseness:** Begriffsstutzigkeit, Unverstand.
6 **self-confident:** selbstsicher.
7 **to reckon s.o. up:** jdn. mustern, sich über jdn. klar werden.
9 **to flare:** lodern, flackern, flammend signalisieren.
10 **to shrink away:** zurückweichen, ausweichen.
11 **to disconcert:** verwirren, verunsichern, aus der Fassung bringen.
12 **suddenness:** Plötzlichkeit.
13 **duck:** Schatz (Kosewort).
14 **wilful:** eigenwillig.
15 **shakily** (adv.): unsicher, bebend.
**to nestle down:** sich anschmiegen.
16 **to bud:** knospen.
17 **to murmur:** murmeln, flüstern.
17 f. **on the point of tears:** den Tränen nahe.

"Well, of course you are, what do you expect?" soothed Anne. It was a joke to Frances that Anne should play elder, almost mother to her. But then, Anne was in her unvexed teens; men were like big dogs to her: while Frances, at twenty-three, suffered a good deal.

The country was intensely morning-still. On the common everything shone beside its shadow, and the hill-side gave off heat in silence. The brown turf seemed in a low state of combustion, the leaves of the oaks were scorched brown. Among the blackish foliage in the distance shone the small red and orange of the village.

The willows in the brook-course at the foot of the common suddenly shook with a dazzling effect like diamonds. It was a puff of wind. Anne resumed her normal position. She spread her knees, and put in her lap a handful of hazel nuts, whity-green leafy things, whose

1 **to soothe:** trösten, beruhigen.
4 **unvexed:** ungestört, unbeeinträchtigt.
5 **a good deal:** sehr, beträchtlich.
6 **intensely** (adv.): intensiv.
8 **to give off:** ausströmen, verbreiten.
9 **combustion:** Verbrennung.
10 **scorched:** verbrannt, versengt, verdorrt.
**blackish:** schwärzlich.
**foliage:** Laub, Blattwerk.
13 **willow:** Weide(nbaum).
**brook-course:** Bachlauf.
14 **dazzling:** glänzend, blendend.
15 **puff of wind:** Windstoß.
**to resume:** wieder aufnehmen, wieder einnehmen.
17 **hazel nut:** Haselnuß.
**whity-green:** weißlich-grün.
**leafy:** blättrig.

one cheek was tanned between brown and pink. These she began to crack and eat. Frances, with bowed head, mused bitterly.

"Eh, you know Tom Smedley?" began the young girl, as she pulled a tight kernel out of its shell.

"I suppose so," replied Frances sarcastically.

"Well, he gave me a wild rabbit what he'd caught, to keep with my tame one – and it's living."

"That's a good thing," said Frances, very detached and ironic.

"Well, it *is*! He reckoned he'd take me to Ollerton Feast, but he never did. Look here, he took a servant from the rectory; I saw him."

"So he ought," said Frances.

"No, he oughtn't! And I told him so. And I told him I should tell you – an' I have done."

Click and snap went a nut between her teeth. She sorted out the kernel, and chewed complacently.

"It doesn't make much difference," said Frances.

"Well, 'appen it doesn't; but I was mad with him all the same."

"Why?"

"Because I was; he's no right to go with a servant."

1 **tanned:** (sonnen)gebräunt.
3 **to muse:** nachsinnen, grübeln.
5 **kernel:** Kern.
6 **sarcastically** (adv.): sarkastisch.
11 f. **Ollerton Feast:** Kirchweih, Jahrmarkt in Ollerton.
13 **rectory:** Pfarrhaus.
17 **click and snap:** lautmalerischer Ausdruck; etwa: knick-knack.
18 **complacently** (adv.): (selbst)zufrieden, behaglich.
20 **'appen:** *happen:* hier: vielleicht.
**mad:** wütend, böse.

"He's a perfect right," persisted Frances, very just and cold.

"No, he hasn't, when he'd said he'd take me."

Frances burst into a laugh of amusement and relief.

"Oh no; I'd forgot that," she said, adding, "and what did he say when you promised to tell me?"

"He laughed and said: 'She won't fret her fat over that.'"

"And she won't," sniffed Frances.

There was silence. The common, with its sere, blonde-headed thistles, its heaps of silent bramble, its brown-husked gorse in the glare of sunshine, seemed visionary. Across the brook began the immense pattern of agriculture, white chequering of barley stubble, brown squares of wheat, khaki patches of pasture, red stripes of fallow, with the woodland and the tiny village dark like ornaments, leading away to the distance, right to

1 **to persist:** beharren.
7 **to fret one's fat** (coll.): sich zu Tode grämen.
9 **to sniff:** naserümpfend, verächtlich sagen.
10 **sere:** dürr, welk.
11 **thistle:** Distel.
**bramble:** Brombeerstrauch, Dornengebüsch.
11 f. **brown-husked:** mit braunen Hülsen.
12 **gorse:** Stechginster.
**glare:** greller Schein.
12 f. **visionary:** visionär, unwirklich.
14 **chequering:** Karomuster.
**barley:** Gerste.
**stubble:** Stoppeln.
15 **khaki:** khakifarben, gelbbraun.
**pasture:** Weideland.
16 **fallow:** Brachland.
**woodland:** Waldung, Waldland.
17 **ornament:** Ornament, Verzierung, Schmuck(stück).

the hills, where the check-pattern grew smaller and smaller, till, in the blackish haze of heat, far off, only the tiny white squares of barley stubble showed distinct.

"Eh, I say, here's a rabbit-hole!" cried Anne suddenly. "Should we watch if one comes out? You won't have to fidget, you know."

The two girls sat perfectly still. Frances watched certain objects in her surroundings: they had a peculiar, unfriendly look about them: the weight of greenish elderberries on their purpling stalks; the twinkling of the yellowing crab-apple that clustered high up in the hedge, against the sky: the exhausted, limp leaves of the primroses lying flat in the hedge-bottom: all looked strange to her. Then her eyes caught a movement. A mole was moving silently over the warm, red soil, nosing, shuffling hither and thither, flat, and dark as a shadow, shifting about, and as suddenly brisk, and as si-

1 **check-pattern:** Karo-, Schachbrettmuster.
2 **haze:** Dunst.
6 **to fidget:** zappeln, unruhig sein.
9 **greenish:** grünlich.
10 **elderberry:** Holunderbeere.
**to purple:** sich purpurn färben.
**stalk:** Stiel.
**twinkling:** Blitzen, Funkeln.
11 **crab-apple:** Holzapfel.
**to cluster:** sich drängen, dicht wachsen.
12 **limp:** schlaff.
13 **primrose:** Primel.
15 **mole:** Maulwurf.
15 f. **to nose:** schnuppern, wittern.
16 **to shuffle:** schlurfen, sich schwerfällig vorwärtsbewegen.
**hither and thither:** hin und her, hierhin und dorthin.
17 **brisk:** lebhaft, flink.

lent, like a very ghost of *joie de vivre*. Frances started, from habit was about to call on Anne to kill the little pest. But, to-day her lethargy of unhappiness was too much for her. She watched the little brute paddling, snuffing, touching things to discover them, running in blindness, delighted to ecstasy by the sunlight and the hot, strange things that caressed its belly and its nose. She felt a keen pity for the little creature.

"Eh, our Fran, look there! It's a mole."

Anne was on her feet, standing watching the dark, unconscious beast. Frances frowned with anxiety.

"It doesn't run off, does it?" said the young girl softly. Then she stealthily approached the creature. The mole paddled fumblingly away. In an instant Anne put her foot upon it, not too heavily. Frances could see the struggling, swimming movement of the little pink hands of the brute, the twisting and twitching of its pointed nose, as it wrestled under the sole of the boot.

1 **joie de vivre** (Fr.): Lebensfreude.
**to start:** zusammenfahren, erschrecken.
3 **pest:** Plage, Schädling.
**lethargy:** Lethargie, Teilnahmslosigkeit, Stumpfheit.
4 **brute:** Tier, vernunftloses Wesen.
**to paddle:** krabbeln, watscheln.
5 **to snuff:** schnüffeln.
6 **ecstasy:** Ekstase, Verzückung.
7 **to caress:** streicheln, liebkosen.
11 **to frown:** die Stirn runzeln.
13 **stealthily** (adv.): verstohlen, heimlich, behutsam.
14 **fumblingly** (adv.): täppisch.
17 **twitching:** Zucken.
18 **to wrestle:** ringen, sich winden.
**sole:** Sohle.

"It *does* wriggle!" said the bonny girl, knitting her brows in a frown at the eerie sensation. Then she bent down to look at her trap. Frances could now see, beyond the edge of the boot-sole, the heaving of the velvet shoulders, the pitiful turning of the sightless face, the frantic rowing of the flat, pink hands.

"Kill the thing," she said, turning away her face.

"Oh – I'm not," laughed Anne, shrinking. "You can, if you like."

"I *don't* like," said Frances, with quiet intensity.

After several dabbing attempts, Anne succeeded in picking up the little animal by the scruff of its neck. It threw back its head, flung its long blind snout from side to side, the mouth open in a peculiar oblong, with tiny pinkish teeth at the edge. The blind, frantic mouth

1 **to wriggle:** sich winden, zappeln.
**bonny:** munter, fröhlich.
1 f. **to knit one's brows in a frown:** die Augenbrauen zu einem mißbilligenden oder sorgenvollen Gesichtsausdruck zusammenziehen, die Stirn runzeln.
2 **eerie:** unheimlich, sonderbar.
4 **heaving:** Heben, Auf-und-ab-Bewegung.
4 f. **velvet:** samten.
5 **pitiful:** mitleiderregend, jämmerlich.
6 **frantic:** wild, rasend, verzweifelt.
**rowing:** Rudern.
8 **to shrink:** zurückschrecken, schaudern, sich scheuen.
10 **intensity:** Intensität, Nachdruck.
11 **to dab:** ab-, betupfen; einen Klaps geben.
12 **scruff of the neck:** Genick.
13 **to fling:** werfen, schleudern.
**snout:** Schnauze.
14 **oblong:** Rechteck.
15 **pinkish:** leicht rötlich, hellrosa.

gaped and writhed. The body, heavy and clumsy, hung scarcely moving.

"Isn't it a snappy little thing," observed Anne, twisting to avoid the teeth.

"What are you going to do with it?" asked Frances sharply.

"It's got to be killed – look at the damage they do. I s'll take it home and let dadda or somebody kill it. I'm not going to let it go."

She swaddled the creature clumsily in her pocket handkerchief and sat down beside her sister. There was an interval of silence, during which Anne combated the efforts of the mole.

"You've not had much to say about Jimmy this time. Did you see him often in Liverpool?" Anne asked suddenly.

"Once or twice," replied Frances, giving no sign of how the question troubled her.

"And aren't you sweet on him any more, then?"

"I should think I'm not, seeing that he's engaged."

"Engaged? Jimmy Barrass! Well, of all things! I never thought *he'd* get engaged."

1 **to gape:** sich weit öffnen.
**to writhe:** sich winden, krümmen, schmerzhaft verziehen.
**clumsy:** schwerfällig, unbeholfen, plump.
3 **snappy:** bissig.
7 **s'll:** *shall.*
8 **dadda:** Papa.
10 **to swaddle:** (ein)wickeln.
12 **to combat s.th.:** etwas bekämpfen, gegen etwas ankämpfen.
19 **to be sweet on s.o.:** in jdn. verliebt sein.
21 **of all things:** ausgerechnet.

Why not, he's as much right as anybody else?" snapped Frances.

Anne was fumbling with the mole.

"'Appen so," she said at length; "but I never thought Jimmy would, though."

"Why not?" snapped Frances.

"*I* don't know – this blessed mole, it'll not keep still! – who's he got engaged to?"

"How should I know?"

"I thought you'd ask him; you've known him long enough. I s'd think he thought he'd get engaged now he's a Doctor of Chemistry."

Frances laughed in spite of herself.

"What's that got to do with it?" she asked.

"I'm sure it's got a bit. He'll want to feel *somebody* now, so he's got engaged. Hey, stop it; go in!"

But at this juncture the mole almost succeeded in wriggling clear. It wrestled and twisted frantically, waved its pointed blind head, its mouth standing open like a little shaft, its big, wrinkled hands spread out.

"Go in with you!" urged Anne, poking the little creature with her forefinger, trying to get it back into the handkerchief. Suddenly the mouth turned like a spark on her finger.

1 **to snap:** scharf, bissig erwidern.
3 **to fumble:** tändeln, herumspielen.
11 **s'd:** *should.*
13 **in spite of herself:** gegen ihren Willen, unwillkürlich.
17 **juncture:** Zeitpunkt, kritischer Moment.
20 **shaft:** Schaft, Stab.
**wrinkled:** faltig, runzlig.
21 **to poke:** stoßen, pieken.
23 **spark:** Funke.

"Oh!" she cried, "he's bit me."

She dropped him to the floor. Dazed, the blind creature fumbled round. Frances felt like shrieking. She expected him to dart away in a flash, like a mouse, and there he remained groping; she wanted to cry to him to be gone. Anne, in a sudden decision of wrath, caught up her sister's walking-cane. With one blow the mole was dead. Frances was startled and shocked. One moment the little wretch was fussing in the heat, and the next it lay like a little bag, inert and black – not a struggle, scarce, a quiver.

"It is dead!" Frances said breathlessly. Anne took her finger from her mouth, looked at the tiny pin-pricks, and said:

"Yes, he is, and I'm glad. They're vicious little nuisances, moles are."

With which her wrath vanished. She picked up the dead animal.

"Hasn't it got a beautiful skin," she mused, stroking the fur with her forefinger, then with her cheek.

"Mind," said Frances sharply. "You'll have the blood on your skirt!"

2 **dazed:** betäubt, verwirrt.
3 **to shriek:** kreischen.
4 **to dart away:** davonschießen, -rennen.
5 **to grope:** tasten, tappen, tastend suchen.
6 **wrath:** Zorn.
7 **walking-cane:** Spazierstock.
8 **startled:** erschreckt, bestürzt, verblüfft.
9 **wretch:** Wicht, Schelm, armer Kerl.
10 **inert:** untätig, unbeweglich.
11 **quiver:** Zucken, Beben.
13 **pin-prick:** Nadelstich.
19 **to stroke:** streicheln.

One ruby drop of blood hung on the small snout, ready to fall. Anne shook it off on to some harebells. Frances suddenly became calm; in that moment, grown-up.

"I suppose they have to be killed," she said, and a certain rather dreary indifference succeeded to her grief. The twinkling crab-apples, the glitter of brilliant willows now seemed to her trifling, scarcely worth the notice. Something had died in her, so that things lost their poignancy. She was calm, indifference overlying her quiet sadness. Rising, she walked down to the brook-course.

"Here, wait for me," cried Anne, coming tumbling after.

Frances stood on the bridge, looking at the red mud trodden into pockets by the feet of cattle. There was not a drain of water left, but everything smelled green, succulent. Why did she care so little for Anne, who was so fond of her? she asked herself. Why did she care so little for anyone? She did not know, but she felt a rather stubborn pride in her isolation and indifference.

1 **ruby:** rubinrot.
2 **harebell:** Glockenblume.
5 **dreary:** trübe, öde.
**indifference:** Gleichgültigkeit.
6 **glitter:** Glitzern, Glänzen, Funkeln.
7 **trifling:** banal, unbedeutend.
9 **poignancy:** Schärfe, Eindringlichkeit, Bitterkeit.
12 **to tumble:** stürzen, stürmen.
15 **pocket:** hier: Loch, Höhlung, Vertiefung.
16 **drain:** Rinnsal, Abfluß.
17 **succulent:** saftig.
20 **stubborn:** störrisch, eigensinnig.

They entered a field where stooks of barley stood in rows, the straight, blonde tresses of the corn streaming on to the ground. The stubble was bleached by the intense summer, so that the expanse glared white. The next field was sweet and soft with a second crop of seeds; thin, straggling clover whose little pink knobs rested prettily in the dark green. The scent was faint and sickly. The girls came up in single file, Frances leading.

Near the gate a young man was mowing with the scythe some fodder for the afternoon feed of the cattle. As he saw the girls he left off working and waited in an aimless kind of way. Frances was dressed in white muslin, and she walked with dignity, detached and forgetful. Her lack of agitation, her simple, unheeding advance made him nervous. She had loved the far-off Jimmy for

1 **stook:** Mandel (Gruppe von aufgestellten Getreidegarben).
2 **tress:** Flechte, Locke; hier: Ährenbüschel.
3 **bleached:** gebleicht.
4 **expanse:** weite Fläche, Ausdehnung.
**to glare:** grell scheinen, leuchten, blenden.
6 **to straggle:** wuchern.
**clover:** Klee.
**knob:** Knopf, Knauf; hier: (runder) Blütenkopf.
8 **sickly:** matt; unangenehm süßlich.
10 **to mow:** mähen.
**scythe:** Sense.
11 **fodder:** Futter.
**feed:** Nahrung, Fütterung.
12 **to leave off doing s.th.:** aufhören, etwas zu tun.
13 **muslin:** Musselin.
14 **forgetful:** achtlos, nachlässig.
15 **agitation:** Erregung, Unruhe.
**unheeding:** sorglos, achtlos.

five years, having had in return his half-measures. This man only affected her slightly.

Tom was of medium stature, energetic in build. His smooth, fair-skinned face was burned red, not brown, by the sun, and this ruddiness enhanced his appearance of good humour and easiness. Being a year older than Frances, he would have courted her long ago had she been so inclined. As it was, he had gone his uneventful way amiably, chatting with many a girl, but remaining unattached, free of trouble for the most part. Only he knew he wanted a woman. He hitched his trousers just a trifle self-consciously as the girls approached. Frances was a rare, delicate kind of being, whom he realized with a queer and delicious stimulation in his veins. She gave him a slight sense of suffocation. Somehow, this morning, she affected him more than usual. She was dressed in white. He, however, being matter-of-fact in his mind, did not realize. His feeling had never become conscious, purposive.

1 **half-measure:** Halbheit, Halbherzigkeit.
2 **to affect s.o.:** jdn. mögen; auf jdn. wirken.
3 **stature:** Statur, Gestalt.
5 **ruddiness:** Röte, rote Gesichtsfarbe.
**to enhance:** erhöhen, verstärken.
8 **uneventful:** ereignislos.
9 **amiably** (adv.): liebenswürdig, freundlich.
**to chat:** plaudern.
11 **to hitch:** hochziehen.
12 **a trifle:** ein wenig, eine Spur.
13 **to realize:** hier auch: sich (in Gedanken) vorstellen.
14 **stimulation:** Reiz, Belebung.
15 **suffocation:** Erstickung, Atembeklemmung.
17 **matter-of-fact:** pragmatisch, sachlich, nüchtern.
19 **purposive:** zielstrebig, zweckbestimmt.

Frances knew what she was about. Tom was ready to love her as soon as she would show him. Now that she could not have Jimmy, she did not poignantly care. Still, she would have something. If she could not have the best – Jimmy, whom she knew to be something of a snob – she would have the second best, Tom. She advanced rather indifferently.

"You are back, then!" said Tom. She marked the touch of uncertainty in his voice.

"No," she laughed, "I'm still in Liverpool," and the undertone of intimacy made him burn.

"This isn't you, then?" he asked.

Her heart leapt up in approval. She looked in his eyes, and for a second was with him.

"Why, what do you think?" she laughed.

He lifted his hat from his head with a distracted little gesture. She liked him, his quaint ways, his humour, his ignorance, and his slow masculinity.

"Here, look here, Tom Smedley," broke in Anne.

"A moudiwarp! Did you find it dead?" he asked.

"No, it bit me," said Anne.

"Oh, aye! An' that got your rag out, did it?"

"No, it didn't!" Anne scolded sharply. "Such language!"

3 **poignantly** (adv.): scharf, brennend.
11 **intimacy:** Intimität, Vertrautheit.
16 **distracted:** zerstreut, verwirrt.
17 **quaint:** sonderbar, drollig.
18 **ignorance:** Unwissenheit, Einfältigkeit.
**masculinity:** Männlichkeit.
20 **moudiwarp** (dial.): Maulwurf.
22 **aye:** freilich, wahrhaftig.
**to get s.o.'s rag out** (coll.): jdn. böse, wütend machen.

"Oh, what's up wi' it?"

"I can't bear you to talk broad."

"Can't you?"

He glanced at Frances.

"It isn't nice," Frances said. She did not care, really. The vulgar speech jarred on her as a rule; Jimmy was a gentleman. But Tom's manner of speech did not matter to her.

"I like you to talk *nicely*", she added.

"Do you," he replied, tilting his hat, stirred.

"And generally you *do*, you know," she smiled.

"I s'll have to have a try," he said, rather tensely gallant.

"What?" she asked brightly.

"To talk nice to you," he said. Frances coloured furiously, bent her head for a moment, then laughed gaily, as if she liked this clumsy hint.

"Eh now, you mind what you're saying," cried Anne, giving the young man an admonitory pat.

"You wouldn't have to give yon mole many knocks like that," he teased, relieved to get on safe ground, rubbing his arm.

"No, indeed, it died in one blow," said Frances, with a flippancy that was hateful to her.

2 **to talk broad:** sich platt, ungehobelt, unfein ausdrücken.
6 **vulgar:** vulgär, gewöhnlich.
10 **to tilt:** schräg rücken, verschieben.
16 **furiously** (adv.): wütend.
19 **admonitory:** ermahnend, warnend.
**pat:** Klaps.
20 **yon mole** (dial.): der Maulwurf da.
21 **to tease:** necken, ärgern.
24 **flippancy:** Leichtfertigkeit, Frivolität, Geschwätzigkeit.

"You're not so good at knockin' 'em?" he said, turning to her.

"I don't know, if I'm cross," she said decisively.

"No?" he replied, with alert attentiveness.

"I could," she added, harder, "if it was necessary."

He was slow to feel her difference.

"And don't you consider it *is* necessary?" he asked, with misgiving.

"W–ell–is it?" she said, looking at him steadily, coldly.

"I reckon it is," he replied, looking away, but standing stubborn.

She laughed quickly.

"But it isn't necessary for *me*," she said, with slight contempt.

"Yes, that's quite true," he answered.

She laughed in a shaky fashion.

"*I know it is*," she said; and there was an awkward pause.

"Why, would you *like* me to kill moles then?" she asked tentatively, after a while.

"They do us a lot of damage," he said, standing firm on his own ground, angered.

"Well, I'll see the next time I come across one," she promised defiantly. Their eyes met, and she sank before him, her pride troubled. He felt uneasy and trium-

4 **alert:** wachsam, auf der Hut.
8 **misgiving:** Befürchtung, Zweifel.
21 **tentatively** (adv.): vorsichtig, zögernd, sondierend.
25 **defiantly** (adv.): trotzig, herausfordernd.
26 f. **triumphant:** triumphierend, frohlockend.

phant and baffled, as if fate had gripped him. She smiled as she departed.

"Well," said Anne, as the sisters went through the wheat stubble; "I don't know what you two's been jawing about, I'm sure."

"Don't you?" laughed Frances significantly.

"No, I don't. But, at any rate, Tom Smedley's a good deal better to my thinking than Jimmy, so there – and nicer."

"Perhaps he is," said Frances coldly.

And the next day, after a secret, persistent hunt, she found another mole playing in the heat. She killed it, and in the evening, when Tom came to the gate to smoke his pipe after supper, she took him the dead creature.

"Here you are then!" she said.

"Did you catch it?" he replied, taking the velvet corpse into his fingers and examining it minutely. This was to hide his trepidation.

"Did you think I couldn't?" she asked, her face very near his.

"Nay, I didn't know."

She laughed in his face, a strange little laugh that caught her breath, all agitation, and tears, and reckless-

1 **baffled:** verblüfft.
8 **so there:** das sag ich dir!
11 **persistent:** ausdauernd, beharrlich.
19 **trepidation:** Beben, Unruhe, Beklommenheit.
22 **nay:** nein.
24 **to catch s.o.'s breath:** jdm. den Atem verschlagen.
24 f. **recklessness:** Verwegenheit.

ness of desire. He looked frightened and upset. She put her hand to his arm.

"Shall you go out wi' me?" he asked, in a difficult, troubled tone.

She turned her face away, with a shaky laugh. The blood came up in him, strong, overmastering. He resisted it. But it drove him down, and he was carried away. Seeing the winsome, frail nape of her neck, fierce love came upon him for her, and tenderness.

"We s'll 'ave to tell your mother," he said. And he stood, suffering, resisting his passion for her.

"Yes," she replied, in a dead voice. But there was a thrill of pleasure in this death.

6 **overmastering:** überwältigend, übermannend.
8 **winsome:** einnehmend, reizend.
**frail:** zart, zerbrechlich.
**nape of the neck:** Nacken.
13 **thrill:** Schauer, Kitzel, Vibration.

Katherine Mansfield

# The Singing Lesson

With despair – cold, sharp despair – buried deep in her heart like a wicked knife, Miss Meadows, in cap and gown and carrying a little baton, trod the cold corridors that led to the music-hall. Girls of all ages, rosy from the air, and bubbling over with that gleeful excitement that comes from running to school on a fine autumn morning, hurried, skipped, fluttered by; from the hollow classrooms came a quick drumming of voices; a bell rang; a voice like a bird cried, "Muriel." And then there came from the staircase a tremendous knock-knock-knocking. Someone had dropped her dumb-bells.

The Science Mistress stopped Miss Meadows.

"Good mor-ning," she cried, in her sweet, affected drawl. "Isn't it cold? It might be win-ter."

Miss Meadows, hugging the knife, stared in hatred at the Science Mistress. Everything about her was sweet,

5 **gown:** Gewand, Talar.
**baton:** Stab, Taktstock.
6 **rosy:** rosig.
7 **gleeful:** fröhlich, lustig.
9 **to flutter:** flattern, wogen.
13 f. **dumb-bell:** Hantel.
16 **affected:** affektiert, geziert.
17 **drawl:** gedehnte, schleppende Sprechweise.

pale, like honey. You would not have been surprised to see a bee caught in the tangles of that yellow hair.

"It is rather sharp," said Miss Meadows, grimly.

The other smiled her sugary smile.

"You look fro-zen," said she. Her blue eyes opened wide; there came a mocking light in them. (Had she noticed anything?)

"Oh, not quite as bad as that," said Miss Meadows, and she gave the Science Mistress, in exchange for her smile, a quick grimace and passed on. . . .

Forms Four, Five and Six were assembled in the music-hall. The noise was deafening. On the platform, by the piano, stood Mary Beazley, Miss Meadow's favourite, who played accompaniments. She was turning the music-stool. When she saw Miss Meadows she gave a loud, warning "Sh-sh! girls!" and Miss Meadows, her hands thrust in her sleeves, the baton under her arm, strode down the centre aisle, mounted the steps, turned sharply, seized the brass music-stand, planted it in front of her, and gave two sharp taps with her baton for silence.

"Silence, please! Immediately!" and, looking at no-

2 **tangle:** Gewirr, Knoten, lose Strähne.
4 **sugary:** süßlich, zuckersüß.
5 **frozen:** (eis)kalt, erfroren, erstarrt.
6 **mocking:** spöttisch.
10 **grimace:** Grimasse.
12 **deafening:** ohrenbetäubend.
14 **accompaniment:** (musikalische) Begleitung.
17 **to thrust:** stecken, schieben.
**to stride:** schreiten.
18 **aisle:** Gang (zwischen Stuhlreihen).
19 **music-stand:** Notenständer, -pult.

body, her glance swept over that sea of coloured flannel blouses, with bobbing pink faces and hands, quivering butterfly hair-bows and music books outspread. She knew perfectly well what they were thinking. "Meady is in a wax." Well, let them think it! Her eyelids quivered; she tossed her head, defying them. What could the thoughts of those creatures matter to someone who stood there bleeding to death, pierced to the heart, to the heart, by such a letter –

... "I feel more and more strongly that our marriage would be a mistake. Not that I do not love you. I love you as much as it is possible for me to love any woman, but, truth to tell, I have come to the conclusion that I am not a marrying man, and the idea of settling down fills me with nothing but –" and the word "disgust" was scratched out lightly and "regret" written over the top. Basil! Miss Meadows stalked over to the piano. And Mary Beazley, who was waiting for this moment, bent forward; her curls fell over her cheeks while she breathed, "Good morning, Miss Meadows," and she motioned towards rather than handed to her mistress

1 **flannel:** Flanell.
2 **to bob:** sich hin und her, auf und ab bewegen, wippen.
**to quiver:** beben, zittern.
4 f. **to be in a wax** (coll.): eine Stinkwut haben, schlechter Laune sein.
6 **to toss one's head:** den Kopf zurückwerfen.
**to defy:** trotzen, herausfordern.
8 **to pierce:** durchbohren.
14 **not to be a marrying man:** kein (geeigneter) Ehekandidat, nicht ehetauglich sein.
15 **disgust:** Abscheu.
17 **to stalk:** stolzieren, schreiten, steif gehen.
21 **to motion:** hier: hinhalten.

a beautiful yellow chrysanthemum. This little ritual of the flower had been gone through for ages and ages, quite a term and a half. It was as much part of the lesson as opening the piano. But this morning, instead of taking it up, instead of tucking it into her belt while she leant over Mary and said, "Thank you, Mary. How very nice! Turn to page thirty-two," what was Mary's horror when Miss Meadows totally ignored the chrysanthemum, made no reply to her greeting, but said in a voice of ice, "Page fourteen, please, and mark the accents well."

Staggering moment! Mary blushed until the tears stood in her eyes, but Miss Meadows was gone back to the music-stand; her voice rang through the music-hall.

"Page fourteen. We will begin with page fourteen. 'A Lament.' Now, girls, you ought to know it by this time. We shall take it all together; not in parts, all together. And without expression. Sing it, though, quite simply, beating time with the left hand."

She raised the baton; she tapped the music-stand twice. Down came Mary on the opening chord; down came all those left hands, beating the air, and in chimed those young, mournful voices:

1 **chrysanthemum:** Chrysantheme.
5 **to tuck:** ein-, feststecken.
12 **staggering:** erschütternd, verblüffend, beunruhigend.
**to blush:** erröten.
16 **lament:** Klage(lied).
17 **part:** (Sing-)Stimme.
21 **chord:** Akkord.
22 **to chime in:** einstimmen, -fallen.
23 **mournful:** trauernd, klagend, düster.

Fast! Ah, too Fast Fade the Ro-o-ses of
Pleasure;
Soon Autumn yields unto Wi-i-nter Drear.
Fleetly! Ah, Fleetly Mu-u-sic's Gay Measure
Passes away from the Listening Ear.

Good heavens, what could be more tragic than that lament! Every note was a sigh, a sob, a groan of awful mournfulness. Miss Meadows lifted her arms in the wide gown and began conducting with both hands. "... I feel more and more strongly that our marriage would be a mistake ..." she beat. And the voices cried: *Fleetly! Ah, Fleetly.* What could have possessed him to write such a letter! What could have led up to it! It came out of nothing. His last letter had been all about a fumed-oak bookcase he had bought for "our" books and a "natty little hall-stand" he had seen, "a very neat affair with a carved owl on a bracket holding three hat-brushes in its claws." How she had smiled at that! So like a man to think one needed three hat-brushes! *From the Listening Ear*, sang the voices.

"Once again," said Miss Meadows. "But this time in

3 **drear:** *dreary:* öde, trostlos.
4 **fleetly** (adv.): flink, flüchtig.
7 **sob:** Schluchzer.
**groan:** Stöhnen.
15 **fumed-oak:** aus dunklem, antik wirkendem Eichenholz.
**bookcase:** Bücherregal, -schrank.
16 **natty:** hübsch, nett, schmuck.
17 **carved:** geschnitzt.
**owl:** Eule.
**bracket:** Konsole.
18 **claw:** Klaue, Kralle.

parts. Still without expression." *Fast! Ah, too Fast.* With the gloom of the contraltos added, one could scarcely help shuddering. *Fade the Roses of Pleasure.* Last time he had come to see her Basil had worn a rose in his buttonhole. How handsome he had looked in that bright blue suit, with that dark red rose! And he knew it too. He couldn't help knowing it. First he stroked his hair, then his moustache; his teeth gleamed when he smiled.

"The headmaster's wife keeps on asking me to dinner. It's a perfect nuisance. I never get an evening to myself in that place."

"But can't you refuse?"

"Oh, well, it doesn't do for a man in my position to be unpopular."

*Music's Gay Measure*, wailed the voices. The willow trees, outside the high, narrow windows, waved in the wind. They had lost half their leaves. The tiny ones that clung wriggled like fishes caught on a line. ". . . I am not a marrying man. . . ." The voices were silent; the piano waited.

"Quite good," said Miss Meadows, but still in such a strange, stony tone that the younger girls began to feel

2 **gloom:** Düsterkeit, Schwermut.
**contralto:** (tiefe) Altstimme.
3 **to shudder:** schaudern.
7 **to stroke:** streichen, streicheln.
8 **moustache:** Schnurrbart.
**to gleam:** strahlen, schimmern.
16 **to wail:** (weh)klagen, jammern.
16 f. **willow tree:** Weide(nbaum).
19 **to wriggle:** sich hin und her bewegen, winden, zappeln.
23 **stony:** steinern, versteinert.

positively frightened. "But now that we know it, we shall take it with expression. As much expression as you can put into it. Think of the words, girls. Use your imaginations. *Fast! Ah, too Fast*," cried Miss Meadows. "That ought to break out – a loud, strong *forte* – a lament. And then in the second line, *Winter Drear*, make that *Drear* sound as if a cold wind were blowing through it. *Dre-ar!*" said she so awfully that Mary Beazley, on the music-stool, wriggled her spine. "The third line should be one crescendo. *Fleetly! Ah, Fleetly Music's Gay Measure.* Breaking on the first word of the last line, *Passes*. And then on the word, *Away*, you must begin to die ... to fade ... until *the Listening Ear* is nothing more than a faint whisper.... You can slow down as much as you like almost on the last line. Now, please."

Again the two light taps; she lifted her arms again. *Fast! Ah, too Fast*. "... and the idea of settling down fills me with nothing but disgust –" Disgust was what he had written. That was as good as to say their engagement was definitely broken off. Broken off! Their engagement! People had been surprised enough that she had got engaged. The Science Mistress would not believe it at first. But nobody had been as surprised as she. She was thirty. Basil was twenty-five. It had been a miracle, simply a miracle, to hear him say, as they walked home from church that very dark night, "You know, somehow or other, I've got fond of you." And he had taken hold of the end of her ostrich feather boa. *Passes away from the Listening Ear.*

9 **spine:** Wirbelsäule.
28 **ostrich feather:** Straußenfeder.

"Repeat! Repeat!" said Miss Meadows. "More expression, girls! Once more!"

*Fast! Ah, too Fast.* The older girls were crimson; some of the younger ones began to cry. Big spots of rain blew against the windows, and one could hear the willows whispering, ". . . not that I do not love you. . . ."

"But, my darling, if you love me," thought Miss Meadows, "I don't mind how much it is. Love me as little as you like." But she knew he didn't love her. Not to have cared enough to scratch out that word "disgust" so that she couldn't read it! *Soon Autumn yields unto Winter Drear.* She would have to leave the school, too. She could never face the Science Mistress or the girls after it got known. She would have to disappear somewhere. *Passes away.* The voices began to die, to fade, to whisper . . . to vanish. . . .

Suddenly the door opened. A little girl in blue walked fussily up the aisle, hanging her head, biting her lips, and twisting the silver bangle on her red little wrist. She came up the steps and stood before Miss Meadows.

"Well, Monica, what is it?"

"Oh, if you please, Miss Meadows," said the little girl, gasping, "Miss Wyatt wants to see you in the mistress's room."

"Very well," said Miss Meadows. And she called to the girls, "I shall put you on your honour to talk quietly

3 **crimson:** dunkel-, karminrot.

18 **fussily** (adv.): hektisch, in verlegener Geschäftigkeit.

19 **bangle:** Armreif, -band.

23 **to gasp:** keuchen.

26 **to put s.o. on his, her honour:** jdn. auf sein Ehrgefühl, seinen Anstand verweisen; sich auf jds. Anstand verlassen.

while I am away." But they were too subdued to do anything else. Most of them were blowing their noses.

The corridors were silent and cold; they echoed to Miss Meadows' steps. The head mistress sat at her desk. For a moment she did not look up. She was as usual disentangling her eyeglasses, which had got caught in her lace tie. "Sit down, Miss Meadows," she said very kindly. And then she picked up a pink envelope from the blotting-pad. "I sent for you just now because this telegram has come for you."

"A telegram for me, Miss Wyatt?"

Basil! he had committed suicide, decided Miss Meadows. Her hand flew out, but Miss Wyatt held the telegram back a moment. "I hope it's not bad news," she said, no more than kindly. And Miss Meadows tore it open.

"Pay no attention to letter must have been mad bought hat-stand to-day Basil," she read. She couldn't take her eyes off the telegram.

"I do hope it's nothing very serious," said Miss Wyatt, leaning forward.

"Oh no, thank you, Miss Wyatt," blushed Miss Meadows. "It's nothing bad at all. It's" – and she gave an apologetic little laugh – "it's from my *fiancé* saying that . . . saying that –" There was a pause. "I *see*," said Miss

1 **subdued:** gedämpft, eingeschüchtert.
3 **to echo:** echoen, widerhallen.
5 f. **to disentangle:** losmachen, entwirren.
7 **lace tie:** Spitzenschleife, -halsbinde.
9 **blotting-pad:** Schreibunterlage.
24 **apologetic:** entschuldigend.
**fiancé:** Verlobter.

Wyatt. And another pause. Then – "You've fifteen minutes more of your class, Miss Meadows, haven't you?"

"Yes, Miss Wyatt." She got up. She half ran towards the door.

"Oh, just one minute, Miss Meadows," said Miss Wyatt. "I must say I don't approve of my teachers having telegrams sent to them in school hours, unless in case of very bad news, such as death," explained Miss Wyatt, "or a very serious accident, or something to that effect. Good news, Miss Meadows, will always keep, you know."

On the wings of hope, of love, of joy, Miss Meadows sped back to the music-hall, up the aisle, up the steps, over to the piano.

"Page thirty-two, Mary", she said, "page thirty-two," and, picking up the yellow chrysanthemum, she held it to her lips to hide her smile. Then she turned to the girls, rapped with her baton: "Page thirty-two, girls. Page thirty-two."

"We come here To-day with Flowers o'erladen,
With baskets of Fruit and Ribbons to boot,
To-oo Congratulate . . ."

"Stop! Stop!" cried Miss Meadows. "This is awful. This is dreadful." And she beamed at her girls. "What's the matter with you all? Think, girls, think of what you're

19 **to rap:** klopfen, pochen.
21 **o'erladen:** *overladen:* überladen.
22 **to boot:** als Zugabe, obendrein.
25 **dreadful:** furchtbar, schrecklich.

*singing. Use your imaginations. With Flowers o'erladen. Baskets of Fruit and Ribbons to boot.* And *Congratulate.*" Miss Meadows broke off. "Don't look so doleful, girls. It ought to sound warm, joyful, eager. *Congratulate.* Once more. Quickly. All together. Now then!" And this time Miss Meadows' voice sounded over all the other voices – full, deep, glowing with expression.

3 **doleful:** kummervoll, trübsinnig.
7 **to glow:** glühen.

Elizabeth Bowen

# The Needlecase

The car was sent to the train – along the straight road between dykes in the late spring dusk – to bring back Miss Fox, who was coming to sew for a week. Frank, the second son of the house, had come suddenly back from town; he was pleased to find the car there, which was more than he hoped, but appalled to see Miss Fox, in black, like a jointed image, stepping in at the back. Frank had, and wished to have, no idea who she was. So he sat in front with the chauffeur, looking glumly left at the willows and dykes flitting by, while Miss Fox, from the back, looked as fixedly out at willows and dykes at the other side of the road. No one spoke. They turned in at the lodge gates and the avenue trees closed in.

When the car drew up at the hall door, Frank got out and shouted. It embarrassed him having come home,

2 **needlecase:** Nadelkästchen, -etui.
4 **dyke:** Damm, Graben.
**dusk:** Abenddämmerung.
8 **appalled:** entsetzt, erschrocken.
9 **jointed image:** Figur mit Gliedern oder Gelenken; Gliederpuppe.
11 **glumly** (adv.): mürrisch, verdrießlich.
12 **willow:** Weide(nbaum).
**to flit:** fliegen, huschen.
15 **lodge gate:** (Pförtner-)Tor (zu einem Gutshof).

and he did not want to explain. His sister Angela, sitting up at her window, heard, shot downstairs and flung her arms round his neck, nearly knocking him over, like far too big a dog, as though he had been away two years instead of two days. This pleasure she over-expressed was perfectly genuine; Angela was effusive because she was often depressed; she could not be bothered being subtle with Frank, whom she knew far too well, and whose chagrins she often shared. So she kept up this rowdy pretence that everything was for the best.

"Had-a-good-time?" she said.

"No."

"I'm sure you did really," said Angela.

"No doubt you know best," said Frank. "Who in God's name's that in there?"

"Oh, that's Miss *Fox*," explained Angela, peering into the car, where Miss Fox sat like an image, waiting to be let out. Angela rang the bell wildly for someone to come and cope. The chauffeur carried Frank's bag and the sewing-woman's strapped-up brown paper suitcase up the wide steps. The front of the house loomed over them, massive and dark and cold: it was the kind of house that easily looks shut up, and, when shut up,

2 **to fling:** werfen, schleudern.
6 **effusive:** überschwenglich.
9 **chagrin:** Kummer, Ärger.
10 **rowdy:** lärmend, grob.
17 **to peer:** gucken, spähen.
20 **to cope:** die Sache in die Hand nehmen, sich (darum) kümmern.
21 **strapped-up:** mit einem Riemen verschnürt.

looks derelict. Angela took Frank's arm and they went indoors, into the billiard-room, the only place they could be certain of meeting nobody else. The room had a dank, baizey smell, and a smell of cold anthracite from the unlit stove: four battered green shades hung low over the sheeted table. It was not cheery in here. Frank sat on the fender-stool with his shoulders up and stared through his sister Angela heavily, uninvitingly. Had he wished to be quite alone he would not, however, have shouted.

"What did you do?" said Angela.

"Nothing special," Frank said. He had been up to London to meet a man who might get him a job if he liked the looks of him, and the man clearly had not. The man had seen Frank to do Arthur a good turn: unfortunately the brothers did not resemble each other. Everyone liked Arthur. And Frank had stayed up in London, and had hoped to stay longer, because of a girl, but that had been a flop too: he had run through his money; that was why he was home. Angela had the good sense to ask no more. Leaning against the table and screwing

1 **derelict:** verlassen, herrenlos, heruntergekommen.
4 **dank:** feucht, dumpf.
**baizey:** Adjektiv zu *baize* ›grüner, flanellartiger Bezugstoff‹.
**anthracite:** Anthrazit, Glanzkohle.
5 **battered:** abgenutzt, ramponiert.
6 **cheery:** heiter, munter.
7 **fender-stool:** Fußbank, Schemel (am Kamin).
8 **heavily** (adv.): hier: niedergeschlagen.
**uninvitingly** (adv.): nicht einladend, abweisend.
19 **flop:** Fehlschlag, Mißerfolg.
**to have run through one's money:** sein Geld durchgebracht haben.

her left-hand white coral ear-ring tighter (she always looked rather well) she said nonchalantly: "The Applebys have been over. Hermione's after Arthur. They want us for tennis on Monday. The vet. came about Reno; he says it's nothing – oh, and mother has heard from Arthur; he's coming down Friday week and bringing his new girl. So then mother wired to hurry on Miss Fox. She's going to make us all over – first the drawing-room covers, then mother's black lace, and then do up Toddy and me – cut about some dresses and run up some tennis frocks. She's our one hope for the summer. No doubt she sews like hell, but we really couldn't look worse. Could we, Frank? I mean, could we?"

"Yes," said Frank. "I mean, no."

"We heard of her through Aunt Doris," said Angela, chatting away. "She's one of the wonderfully brave – she's got a child to support that she shouldn't have. She trained somewhere or other, so I suppose she *can* make. She's been on these rounds for years, going down in the world a bit. She seems dirt cheap, so there must be something fishy. She used to work, years ago,

1 **coral:** Korallen-.
2 **nonchalantly** (adv.): nonchalant, lässig, ungezwungen.
4 **vet.:** Kurzform von *veterinary surgeon:* Tierarzt.
8 **to make s.th. all over:** etwas ganz umändern, aufarbeiten.
8 f. **drawing-room covers:** Wohnzimmerbezüge.
9 **lace:** (Stoff-)Spitze; Spitzenkleid.
10 **to cut about:** zerschnippeln, zurechtschneiden.
**to run up:** (schnell) zurechtmachen, anfertigen.
11 **frock:** Kleid.
16 **to chat:** plaudern, schwatzen.
19 f. **to go down in the world:** sich verschlechtern, herunterkommen.
20 **dirt cheap:** spottbillig.
21 **fishy:** dubios, verdächtig, faul.

for the Fotheringhams, but Aunt Doris only got on to her after she fell."

"You surprise me," said Frank, yawning drearily, wanting a drink more than anything in the world.

Miss Fox's arrival, though perfectly unassuming, had left quite a wake of noise: she had been taken up and put somewhere, but doors went on opening and shutting, Frank's mother stood out in the hall giving directions, and his elder sister Toddy began shouting for Angela. As Frank crossed the hall his mother broke off to give him her vivid mechanical smile and say, "Oh, you're *back*."

The house – far too big but kept on for Arthur, who was almost always away but liked to think of it there – had many high windows and a white stone well staircase that went, under a skylight, up and up and up. This would have been an excellent house for someone else to have lived in, and heated; Frank and Angela could then have visited comfortably there. As it was, it was like a disheartened edition of Mansfield Park. The country around it was far too empty and flat.

Miss Fox was not to work tonight; they left her to settle in. But Toddy was in such a hurry to get in first with her things that she slipped upstairs, unobtrusively, as soon

1 f. **to get on to s.o.:** mit jdm. Kontakt aufnehmen.
3 **drearily** (adv.): trübsinnig, gelangweilt.
5 **unassuming:** anspruchslos, bescheiden.
11 **vivid:** lebhaft.
14 **well staircase:** Wendeltreppe.
15 **skylight:** Oberlicht.
18 f. **disheartened:** entmutigt, verzagt.
19 **Mansfield Park:** Herrenhaus im gleichnamigen Roman von Jane Austen (1775–1817).
23 **unobtrusively** (adv.): unaufdringlich, unauffällig.

as dinner was over. She found Miss Fox still smoking over her supper tray. She was of that difficult class that has to have trays all the time. Too grand for the servants, she had to be fed in her room – one of those top bedrooms in any Georgian house with high ceilings and windows down by the floor. It looked rather bleak in the light of two hanging bulbs. A massive cheval glass, brought from downstairs today, reflected Miss Fox's figure sitting upright at the table. Deal presses stood round the walls, dress-boxes tottered in stacks and two dressmaker's dummies – one stout and one slimmer – protruded their glazed black busts. A sewing-machine with a treadle awaited the dressmaker's onslaught. In the grate, a thin fire rather uncertainly flapped. What should be done had been done to acclimatize Miss Fox. But her purpose here could be never far from her

3 **grand:** vornehm, in gehobener gesellschaftlicher Position.
5 **Georgian:** georgianisch, aus der Zeit der Könige Georg I.–IV. (1740–1830).
6 **bleak:** öde, kahl, ungemütlich.
7 **cheval glass:** Drehspiegel.
9 **deal press:** Wäscheschrank aus Kiefernholz.
10 **to totter:** schwanken.
**stack:** Stapel.
11 **dressmaker's dummy:** Schneiderpuppe, -büste.
**stout:** füllig, kräftig, gedrungen.
12 **to protrude:** vorstrecken, herausschieben.
**glazed:** satiniert, glänzend.
**bust:** Büste, Busen.
13 **treadle:** Tretkurbel, Pedal, Fußantrieb.
**onslaught:** Angriff, Ansturm.
14 **grate:** Kamin(gitter).
**to flap:** sich hin und her bewegen.
15 **to acclimatize:** akklimatisieren, eingewöhnen.

mind, for she rigidly sat at the table where she would work. A folded-back magazine was propped on the coffee-pot: when Toddy came in she lifted her eyes from this slowly, but did not attempt to rise. Her meek, strong, narrow, expressionless face, with heavy eyelids, high cheekbones and secretive mouth, framed in dusty fair hair brushed flat and knotted behind, looked carven under the bleak overhead light. Its immobile shadows were startling. Toddy thought: "She's important." But this was absurd.

Toddy kicked the door to behind her and stood stock still, a cascade of tired dance dresses flung over one arm, two bales of gingham for tennis frocks balanced under the other. Success this forthcoming summer was deadly important, for Toddy was now twenty-four. She felt Miss Fox held her fate in the palm of her hand. So she stood stock still and did not know how to begin. She had quieter manners, a subtler air than Angela, but was in fact a rather one-idea girl.

1 **rigidly** (adv.): steif, starr.
2 **to prop:** stützen, lehnen.
5 **meek:** sanft, mild, bescheiden.
6 **cheekbone:** Wangenknochen.
**secretive:** verschwiegen.
8 **carven:** geschnitzt, gemeißelt.
**overhead light:** Deckenlicht, -beleuchtung.
9 **immobile:** unbeweglich.
**to startle:** erschrecken, bestürzen.
11 **to kick s.th. to** (coll.): etwas zustoßen, mit einem Tritt schließen.
11 f. **stock still:** regungslos.
12 **cascade:** Kaskade, Wasserfall.
**tired:** hier: abgetragen, verschlissen.
13 **bale:** Ballen.
**gingham:** Gingan (gemusterter Baumwollstoff).

"I hope you have all you want," she said helplessly.

"Yes, thank you, Miss Forrester."

"I mustn't disturb you tonight. But I thought you might like some idea —"

"Show me," said Miss Fox politely, and pushed her chair back from the table.

"My red tulle is ripped right round. It caught on a spur —"

She stopped, for Miss Fox was looking at her so oddly, as though she were a ghost, as though it were terror and pleasure to see her face. Toddy's looks were not startling, but were, like her brother Arthur's, pleasant enough. No one, no man, had been startled this way before.

"It caught on a spur," she said, on a rising note.

Miss Fox's eyes went quite blank. "Tch-tch-tch," she said, and bent quickly over the stuff. She had unpacked and settled in – Toddy saw, looking round – screens hid her bed and washstand, the facts of her life, away, but one or two objects had appeared on the mantelpiece, and a fine, imposing work-basket stood at her elbow. Toddy, who loved work-baskets, had a touch of the jackdaw, so, while Miss Fox was examining the martyred red dress, she flicked back the hinged lid of

7 **tulle:** Tüll(kleid).
**ripped:** zerrissen, aufgerissen.
20 **mantelpiece:** Kaminsims.
21 **imposing:** imposant.
23 **jackdaw:** Dohle.
23 f. **martyred:** ge-, zermartert.
24 **to flick back:** (schnell) zurück-, aufklappen.
**hinged:** mit Scharnieren befestigt.

the basket and with innocent, bird-like impertinence routed through its contents. All sorts of treasures were here; "souvenir" tape-measures, tight velvet emery bags, button-bags, a pin-cushion inside a shell, scissors of all sorts in scabbards – and oh, such a needlecase! "As large as a family Bible," said Toddy, opening it, pleased. And, like a family Bible, it had a photo stuck inside. "Oh, what a nice little boy!" – "*Thank you*," exclaimed Miss Fox, and with irresistible quickness, a snatch, had the needlecase back. The movement so surprising, it seemed not to have happened.

"That looked such a dear little boy," Toddy went on, impenitent.

"My little nephew," Miss Fox said impenetrably.

It was odd to think she had a child, for with such a nun-like face she had looked all wrong, somehow, smoking a cigarette. The dusty look of her hair must be the effect of light, for Toddy, standing above her, looked down and saw how well brushed her hair was. Her fingers looked as though they would always be cold, and Toddy dreaded their touch on her naked spine when the time would come to try on her evening

1 **impertinence:** Dreistigkeit, Unverschämtheit.
2 **to rout:** wühlen, stöbern.
3 **tape-measure:** Meßband, Bandmaß.
**velvet:** samten, aus Samt.
**emery bag:** Schmirgelbeutel.
5 **scabbard:** Schutzhülle.
9 **irresistible:** unwiderstehlich.
10 **snatch:** Schnappen, schneller Zugriff.
13 **impenitent:** ohne Reue, unbußfertig.
14 **impenetrably** (adv.): undurchdringlich, unergründlich.
22 **spine:** Rückgrat, Wirbelsäule.

dresses. And felt frightened alone with her, at the top of this dark, echoing house. They saved light everywhere, you had to grope up the stairs, for this well of a house drank money. So its daughters, likely to wither, had few "advantages". Everyone knew, Arthur knew, that Arthur must marry money. Toddy was sick of the sacrifice. She was in love this year, baulked all the time, and her serene, squarish face concealed a constant, pricking anxiety.

"I've *got* to look nice," she said suddenly.

"I'll do all I can," said Miss Fox, flashing up once again that odd, reminiscent look.

"How *like* you, Toddy," Angela cried at breakfast.

"What was like Toddy?" Frank asked, scrawling a maze among the crumbs by his plate. He seldom listened to what his sisters were saying, but sat on at table with them because he had nowhere special to go next.

"Creeping up there, then poking about in her things. You really might give the poor old creature a break."

2 **to echo:** widerhallen.
3 **to grope up:** sich herauftasten.
4 **to wither:** welken, verdorren, verblühen.
7 **to baulk:** ausweichen, sich entziehen.
8 **serene:** heiter, gelassen.
**squarish:** nahezu eckig.
**to conceal:** verbergen.
12 **reminiscent:** sich erinnernd, nostalgisch.
14 **to scrawl:** kritzeln, (unordentlich) zeichnen.
**maze:** Labyrinth, Irrgarten.
15 **crumb:** Krümel.
18 **to poke about:** herumstochern, -stöbern, -schnüffeln.
19 **to give s.o. a break:** jdn. in Ruhe lassen.

"She's not so old," said Toddy, serene. "And the child looked about seven."

"What was it like?"

"I only saw curls and a collar – I tell you, she snatched it away."

"What child?" said Frank. He pushed his cup across vaguely and Angela gave him more coffee, but it was cold.

"The child she had," said Toddy.

"Oh God," said Frank, "is she fallen?" But he did not care in the least.

"I told you she was, last night," said Angela, hurt.

That morning, Miss Fox was put in the drawing-room to work. Bales of chintz were unrolled and she cut out the new covers, shaping them over the backs of the chairs with pins. In cold, windy April sunlight she crawled round and round the floor, with pins in her mouth. The glazed chintz looked horribly cold. Frank, kept so short of money, not only thought the rosy-and-scrolly pattern itself obscene, but found these new covers a frenzied extravagance. But now Arthur's most promising girl was coming to stay, and must at all costs be impressed. If she did marry Arthur, she'd scrap these covers first thing. Any bride would. Frank leaned

4 f. **to snatch s.th. away:** etwas wegschnappen, entreißen.
14 **chintz:** Chintz (Baumwollgewebe mit glänzender Oberfläche).
19 f. **rosy-and-scrolly pattern:** verschnörkeltes Rosenmuster.
20 **obscene:** obszön, anstößig, widerwärtig.
21 **frenzied:** wahnsinnig.
23 **to scrap:** ausrangieren, auf den Müll tun.
24 **first thing:** zuallererst, als erstes.

in the doorway, letting a draught in that rustled under the chintz, to watch Miss Fox at work on her thankless task. She magnetized his idleness. Their silence was fascinating, for if he spoke she would have to spit out those pins. The drawing-room was full of tables covered with photographs: Arthur at every age. He watched Miss Fox dodge the tables and drag her lengths of chintz clear.

Then she sat back on her heels. "How fast you get on," Frank said.

"I give my whole mind to it."

"Don't your hands get cold, touching that stuff?"

"They may do; I'm not particular."

She put pins back in her mouth and Frank wondered how she had ever been seduced. He picked up her big scissors idly and snipped at the air with them. "This house is like ice," he said. "Do you know this part of the world?"

She was round at the back of the sofa and nothing came for some time; she must be eyeing the pattern and chewing the pins. Then her voice came over the top. "I've heard speak of it. It seems very quiet round here."

"*Quiet* —" began Frank.

But, hearing his voice, his mother looked in and said

1 **to rustle:** rascheln.
3 **to magnetize:** magnetisch anziehen.
7 **to dodge:** ausweichen, umgehen.
11 **to give one's whole mind to s.th.:** sich ganz auf etwas konzentrieren, etwas mit großem Eifer tun.
15 **to seduce:** verführen.
16 **to snip:** schnippeln, schneiden.

with her ready smile: “Come, Frank, I want you a moment. We mustn’t disturb Miss Fox.”

That same afternoon, the sun went in. Sharp dark clouds with steely white edges began bowling over the sky and their passing made the whole landscape anxious and taut. Frank went out riding with Angela; the wind, coming up and up, whistled among the willows; the dykes cut the country up with uneasy gleams. The grass was still fawn-coloured; only their own restlessness told them that it was spring. It *was* quiet round here. They jogged tamely along, and Angela said she saw no reason why things should ever happen, and yet they did. She wished they saw more of life. Even Miss Fox in the house was *something*, she said, something to talk about, something going on. “And of course I do need those clothes. But when we *are* all dressed up, I don’t know where we’re to go. Oh hell, Frank. I mean, really.” She rode hatless, the wind stung her cheeks pink: Frank bitterly thought that she looked like some Academy picture about the Morning of Life.

“Do you think Arthur’ll marry that girl?”

“I daresay he’ll try,” said Frank.

“Oh, come. You know, Frank, our Arthur’s a big suc-

4 **steely:** stählern, Stahl-.
6 **taut:** angespannt, straff.
8 **gleam:** Schimmer.
9 **fawn-coloured:** rehbraun.
9 f. **restlessness:** Unruhe, Rastlosigkeit.
11 **to jog:** trotten, schwerfällig traben.
20 **Academy:** gemeint ist die Royal Academy of Painting, Sculpture and Architecture bzw. deren jährliche Ausstellung.

cess ... It's terrible how we wonder about Miss Fox. Do you think we are getting prurient minds? But the idea's fantastic."

"Fantastic," Frank agreed, feeling his own despondency ironed into him. Angela shot off and galloped across the field.

That night, in a wind direct from the Ural mountains, the house began to creak and strain like a ship. The family sat downstairs with as few lights on as possible. It was Angela who slipped up to talk to Miss Fox. The handsome work-basket was present but hasped shut, and Angela, honourably, turned her eyes from it. She really did want to talk. She sat on the rug by the grate; the wind puffed down the chimney occasional gusts of smoke that made her eyes smart. Miss Fox sat at the table, puffing away at a cigarette with precision. Perhaps she was glad of company. Nothing showed she was not. Her head, sculptured by shadows, was one of the finest heads that Angela had ever seen.

"You must see a lot of funny things, going from house to house."

"Well yes, I do. I do see some funny things."

"Of course, so do hospital nurses. But people must be

2 **prurient:** lüstern.
4 f. **despondency:** Verzagtheit, Mutlosigkeit.
8 **to creak:** knarren.
11 **hasped shut:** mit einem Schließhaken, einer Spange oder einem Schnappschloß verschlossen.
12 **honourably** (adv.): ehrenhaft, anständig.
14 **to puff:** blasen, pusten.
**gust:** Bö.
18 **sculptured:** gemeißelt, geformt.

much funnier trying on clothes. And some families are mares' nests. I wish you'd tell me . . ."

"Oh well, that would hardly do."

"You know nurses aren't discreet . . . My brother Frank thinks you're a witch."

"Gentlemen will have their fun," said Miss Fox, with an odd inflection, as though she were quoting. Meeting Angela's eye, she smiled her held-in, rigid smile. Angela thought with impatience of gentlemen's fun that they must have – and, in this connection, of Arthur, who had his share. She heard the wind gnaw at the corners of this great tomb of a house that he wouldn't let them give up.

"It's all right for Arthur," she said.

"Those photographs in the drawing-room – they are all your Mr. Arthur?"

"Of course," said Angela crossly.

"Miss Toddy favours him, doesn't she?"

Angela hugged her knees and Miss Fox got no answer to this. So the sewing-woman reached out her cold hand across the table, shook out of the packet and lit with precision another thin cigarette. Then: "I've seen Mr. Arthur," she said.

"Oh yes, I've seen Mr. Arthur. He was staying one time

2 **mare's nest:** Windei, Blendwerk.
4 **discreet:** diskret, taktvoll.
5 **witch:** Hexe, Zauberin.
7 **inflection:** Modulation, Betonung.
8 **held-in:** beherrscht, verhalten, gezügelt.
9 **impatience:** Ungeduld, Verärgerung.
11 **to gnaw:** nagen.
12 **tomb:** Grab.

in a lady's house where I worked. There were several young gentlemen there, and I wasn't, of course, in the way of hearing their names. They were a big party, ever so gay and high-spirited, dodging all over the house, they used to be, every night, and in and out of my workroom, playing some game. I used to be sitting alone, like I sit here, and they used to stop for a word as they went through, or sometimes get me to hide them. Pleasant, they all were. But I never did catch any names. Mr. Arthur took a particular fancy to one of my dummies, and asked me to lend it him to dress up for some game. I should have known better; I ought to have known my place.

But it was eight years ago. The last night, I let him take the dummy away. They did laugh, I heard. But there was an accident and Mr. Arthur let it drop on the stairs. The pedestal broke and some of the skirt-wires bent. He came back, later, to tell me how sorry he was. He *was* sorry, too. He said he'd make it all right. But he went off next day, and I suppose something happened to put it out of his head. My lady was not at all pleased, as she had had the dummy made to her own figure, and her figure was difficult. I didn't work there again."

"How like him!" exclaimed his sister, savagely reclasping her hands round her knees.

2 f. **to be in the way of doing s.th.:** die Möglichkeit haben, in der Lage sein, etwas zu tun.

4 **high-spirited:** lebhaft, temperamentvoll.
**to dodge:** herumsausen, -flitzen.

17 **pedestal:** Ständer.
**skirt-wires** (pl.): Drahtgeflecht in Paßform des Rockes.

24 f. **to reclasp:** wieder schließen, umklammern.

Miss Fox, immensely collected, let out a cloud of smoke. "He meant no harm," she said stonily.

Frank came upstairs in the dark, feeling his way by the handrail and calling, "Angela?" It gave him the creeps when anyone disappeared. And downstairs Toddy was fumbling on the piano. "Here," called Angela. Frank knocked once, and came in. "You look very snug," he said, rather resentfully. This room's being inhabited gave the house a new focus. Soon they would all be up here. He came and stood by the fire and watched his sister rocking and hugging her knees. He saw by her face that he had cut in on a talk. His own superfluity bit him.

"Miss Fox once knew Arthur, Frank."

"A ladder's run right down your stocking," said Frank with angry irrelevance.

"Damn," said Angela vaguely.

"Best catch it up," said Miss Fox.

She looked from Frank to Angela. There was a pause. Then, in the most businesslike way, she put down her cigarette, opened her work-basket, glanced at Angela's

1 **collected:** beherrscht, gefaßt, ruhig.
2 **stonily** (adv.): versteinert, starr, eisig.
4 **handrail:** Geländer.
6 **to fumble:** hier: herumklimpern.
7 **snug:** gemütlich, behaglich.
8 **resentfully** (adv.): ärgerlich, empfindlich.
**inhabited:** bewohnt.
9 **focus:** Brennpunkt, Mittelpunkt.
12 **superfluity:** Überflüssigkeit.
15 **ladder:** Laufmasche.
16 **irrelevance:** Irrelevanz, Belanglosigkeit.

stocking and, matching it with her eye, drew a strand from a mixed plait of darning silks. Then she took out the big black needlecase. "Mr. Frank . . ." she said. He went over and, taking the case, brought it across to Angela. She knelt upon the hearthrug; he rested a hand on her shoulder and felt the shoulder go stiff. "What a lot of needles," she said mechanically. She and Frank both stared at the photograph of the child. They saw, as Toddy had seen, its curls and its collar. Like Arthur's collar and curls in old photographs downstairs. And between the collar and curls, Arthur's face stared back again at the uncle and aunt.

"I should take a number five needle," said Miss Fox calmly.

"I have," said Angela, closing the needlecase.

"Ladders down stockings break one's heart," said Miss Fox.

1 **strand:** Faden.
2 **plait:** Zopf, geflochtenes Bündel.
**darning silk:** Stopfgarn, Nähseide.
5 **hearthrug:** Kaminvorleger.

Frank O’Connor

# Judas

“Sure you won’t be late, Jerry?” the mother said and I going out.

“Am I ever late?” I said, and I laughed.

That was all we said, but it stuck in my mind. As I was going down the road I was thinking it was months since I’d taken her to the pictures. Of course, you might think that funny, but after the father’s death we were thrown together a lot. And I knew she hated being alone in the house after dark.

At the same time I had my own troubles. You see, being an only child I never knocked round the way other fellows did. All the fellows in the office went with girls, or at any rate let on that they did. They said: “Who was the old doll I saw you with the other night, Jerry? You’d better mind yourself, or you’ll be getting into trouble.” To hear them talk, you’d imagine there was no sport in the world only girls, and that they’d always be getting you into trouble. Paddy Kinnane, for instance, always talked like that, and he never saw how it upset me. I think he thought it a great compliment. It

8 **pictures** (pl.): Kino.

13 **to knock round:** ausgehen, sich die Zeit vertreiben, Vergnügungen nachgehen.

15 **to let on:** so tun (als ob), vorgeben.

wasn't until years after that I began to suspect that Paddy's acquaintance with girls was about of one kind with my own.

Then I met Kitty Doherty. Kitty was a hospital nurse, and all the chaps in the office said a fellow should never go with hospital nurses. Ordinary girls were bad enough, but nurses were a fright – they knew too much. When I met Kitty Doherty I knew that this was a lie. She was a well-educated, superior girl; she lived up the river in a posh locality, and her mother was on all sorts of councils and committees. Kitty was small and wiry; a good-looking girl, always in good humour, and when she talked, she hopped from one subject to another like a robin on a frosty morning. I used to meet her in the evening up the river road, as though I were walking there by accident and very surprised to see her. "Fancy meeting you!" I'd say or, "Well, well, isn't this a great surprise!" Mind you, it usually was, because no matter how much I was expecting her, I was never prepared for the shock of her presence. Then we'd stand talking for half an hour and I'd see her home. Several times she asked me in, but I was too nervous. I knew I'd lose my head, break the china, use some dirty word, and then go home and cut my throat. Of course, I never

5 **chap:** Kerl, Bursche.
7 **fright:** Schrecken, Horror.
10 **posh:** elegant, fein.
**locality:** Gegend, Wohngebiet.
11 **committee:** Komitee, Ausschuß.
**wiry:** drahtig.
13 **to hop:** hüpfen, springen.
14 **robin:** Rotkehlchen.

asked her to come to the pictures or anything of the sort. She was above all that. My only hope was that if I waited long enough I might be able to save her from drowning or the white slavers or something else dramatic, that would show in a modest and dignified way how I felt about her. At the same time I had a bad conscience because I knew I should stay at home more with the mother, but the very thought that I might be missing an opportunity of fishing Kitty out of the river would spoil a whole evening for me.

That night in particular I was nearly distracted. I had not seen Kitty for three weeks. I was sure that, at the very least, she was dying and asking for me, but that no one knew my address. A week before, I had felt I simply couldn't bear it any longer and made an excuse to go down to the post office. I rang up the hospital and asked for Kitty. I fully expected them to say in gloomy tones that Kitty had died half an hour before, and had the shock of my life when the girl at the other end asked my name. I lost my head. "I'm afraid I'm a stranger to Miss Doherty," I said with an embarrassed laugh. "But I have a message for her from a friend."

Then I became completely panic-stricken. What could a girl like Kitty make of a damned, deliberate lie like that? What else was it but a trap laid by an old and cunning hand? I held the receiver out and looked at it

4 **white slaver:** Mädchenhändler.
5 **dignified:** würdig.
11 **distracted:** verstört, rasend.
17 **gloomy:** düster, trübsinnig.
23 **panic-stricken:** von panischem Schrecken ergriffen.
26 **cunning:** schlau, gerissen.

as if it were someone whose neck I was just going to wring. "Moynihan," I said to it, "you're mad. An asylum, Moynihan, is the only place for you."

I heard Kitty's voice, not in my ear at all, but in the telephone booth as though she were standing there with me, and I nearly dropped the receiver in terror. Then I raised it and asked in what I thought of as a French accent: "Who is dat speaking please?" "This is Kitty Doherty," she replied impatiently. "Who are you?"

That was exactly what I was wondering myself. Who the blazes was I? "I am Monsieur Bertrand," I said cautiously. "I am afraid I have the wrong number. I am so sorry." Then I put down the receiver and thought how nice it would be if only I had a penknife handy to cut my throat. It's funny, but from the moment I met Kitty I was always coveting sharp things like razors and penknives. It didn't seem to me that there were enough of them in the world at all.

After that an awful idea dawned on me. Of course, I should have thought of it sooner, but, as you can see, I was not exactly knowledgeable where girls were concerned. I began to see that I was not meeting Kitty for

2 **to wring:** drücken, winden, umdrehen.
2 f. **asylum:** (Irren-)Anstalt.
5 **telephone booth:** Telefonzelle.
9 **impatiently** (adv.): ungeduldig.
11 f. **who the blazes?** (coll.): wer zum Teufel?
15 **penknife:** Feder-, Taschenmesser.
**to have s.th. handy:** etwas zur Hand, greifbar, griffbereit haben.
17 **to covet:** begehren.
22 **knowledgeable:** kenntnisreich, gut unterrichtet.

the very good reason that Kitty did not want to meet me. What her objection was I could only imagine, but then imagination was my strong point. I examined my conscience to see what I might have said to upset her. I remembered every single remark I had made without exception, and unfortunately it was only too clear what her objection was because every single one was either brutal, indecent or disgusting. I had talked of Paddy Kinnane as a fellow who "went with dolls". What could a pure-minded girl think of a chap who naturally used such an expression except – what unfortunately was quite true – that he had a mind like a cesspit.

But this evening I felt more confident. It was a lovely summer evening with views of hillsides and fields between the gaps in the houses, and it raised my spirits. Perhaps I was wrong; perhaps she had not noticed or understood my filthy conversation; perhaps we might meet and walk home together. I walked the full length of the river road and back, and then started to walk it again. The crowds were thinning out as fellows and girls slipped off up the lanes or down the river-bank, courting. As the streets went out like lamps about me my hopes sank lower. I saw clearly that she was avoiding me because she knew that I was not the quiet, good-natured fellow I let on to be but a volcano of

8 **indecent:** unanständig.
**disgusting:** ekelhaft, abstoßend.
12 **cesspit:** Jauchegrube.
14 **hillside:** Hang.
17 **filthy:** schmutzig, dreckig, unflätig.
25 **good-natured:** freundlich, gutmütig, gutwillig.
**volcano:** Vulkan.

brutality and lust. "Lust! lust! lust!" I hissed to myself, clenching my fists. I could have forgiven myself anything but the lust.

Then I glanced up and saw her on top of a tram. I instantly forgot about the lust and smiled and waved my cap at her, but she was looking ahead and did not see me. At least, I hoped she didn't see me. I raced after the tram, intending to jump on to it, sit in one of the back seats on top where she would not notice me, and then say in astonishment as she got off: "Fancy meeting you here." But as if the driver knew exactly what was in my mind, he put on speed, and the old tram went bucketing and screeching down the one straight bit of road in the whole town, and I stood panting in the roadway, smiling as though missing a tram were the best joke in the world, and wishing all the time that I had a penknife and the courage to use it. My position was hopeless!

Then I must have gone a bit mad – really mad, I mean – because I started to race the tram. There were still a lot of people out walking, and they stared after me in an incredulous way, so I lifted my fists to my chest in the attitude of a professional runner and dropped into what I hoped would look like a comfortable stride and

1 **lust:** Wollust, Begierde.
**to hiss:** zischen.
2 **to clench one's fists:** die Fäuste ballen.
13 **to bucket:** rasen, rumpeln.
**to screech:** kreischen.
14 **to pant:** keuchen, japsen.
15 **roadway:** Fahrbahn.
22 **incredulous:** ungläubig, skeptisch.
24 **stride:** Schritt, Gangart.

delude them into the belief that I was training for a big race. By the time I was finished, I *was* a runner, and full of indignation against the people who still continued to stare at me.

Between my running and the tram's halts I just managed to keep it in view as far as the other side of town. When I saw Kitty get off and go up a hilly street I collapsed and was only able to drag myself after her. When she went into a house on the terrace above the road I sat on the high curb with my head between my knees till the panting stopped. At least, I had run her to earth. I could afford to rest and walk up and down before the house till she came out and then say with an innocent smile: "Fancy meeting you!"

But my luck was dead out that night. As I walked up and down, close enough to the house to keep it in view but not close enough to be seen from the windows, I saw a tall man strolling up at the opposite side of the road and my heart sank. It was Paddy Kinnane.

"Hallo, Jerry," he chuckled with that knowing grin he put on whenever he wanted to compliment you on being discovered in a compromising situation. "What are you doing here?"

1 **to delude:** täuschen, verleiten.
3 **indignation:** Entrüstung, Empörung.
5 **halt:** Haltestelle.
7 f. **to collapse:** zusammenbrechen.
10 **curb** (auch: *kerb*): Bordstein(kante).
11 f. **to run s.o. to earth:** jdn. aufstöbern, bis zu seinem Bau, Versteck verfolgen (Jägersprache).
18 **to stroll:** schlendern, bummeln.
20 **to chuckle:** glucksen, leise lachen.

"Just waiting for a chap I had a date with, Paddy," I said trying to sound casual.

"Looks more to me as if you were waiting for an old doll," Paddy said flatteringly. "Still waters run deep. When were you supposed to meet him?"

Cripes, I didn't even know what the time was!

"Half eight," I said at random.

"Half eight?", said Paddy. "Tis nearly nine now."

"Ah, he's a most unpunctual fellow," I said angrily. "He's always the same. He'll turn up all right."

"I may as well wait with you," said Paddy, leaning against the wall and taking out a packet of cigarettes. "You might find yourself stuck at the end of the evening. There's people in this town who have no consideration for anyone."

That was Paddy all out – a heart of gold, no trouble too much for him if he could do you a good turn – I'd have loved to strangle him. I knew there was nothing for it but to make a fresh start.

"Ah, to hell with him!" I said impatiently. "I won't bother waiting any longer. It only struck me this minute that I have another appointment – up the Western Road. You'll excuse me now, Paddy. I'll tell you about it another time."

And back I went to the tramline. I caught a tram and went on to the farther terminus, near Kitty's house.

4 **flatteringly** (adv.): schmeichelnd, schmeichlerisch, schmeichelhaft(erweise).
6 **cripes** (coll.): Mensch!, Mann!
16 **all out:** ganz und gar, durch und durch, typisch.
18 **to strangle:** erwürgen.
18 f. **there was nothing for it but:** es blieb nichts andres übrig als.

There, at least, Paddy Kinnane could not get at me. I sat on the river wall in the dusk. The moon was rising, and every fifteen minutes a tram came grunting and squeaking over the old bridge and went black-out as the conductor switched his trolley. Each time I got off the wall and stood on the kerb in the moonlight, searching for Kitty among the passengers. Then a policeman came along, and, as he seemed suspicious of me, I slunk slowly off up the hill and stood against a wall in shadow. There was a high wall at the other side of the road, and behind it the roof of a house was cut out of the sky in moonlight. Every now and then a tram came in and people passed, and the snatches of conversation I caught were like the warmth from an open door to the heart of a homeless man. It was quite clear now that my position was hopeless. If Kitty had walked or been driven she would have reached home from the opposite direction. She could be at home in bed by now. The last tram came and went, and still there was no Kitty, and still I hung on despairingly. While one glimmer of a chance remained I could not go home.

Then I heard a woman's step. I could not even pretend to myself that it might be Kitty till she suddenly shuf-

2 **dusk:** Abenddämmerung.
3 **to grunt:** grunzen, ächzen.
4 **to squeak:** quietschen, kreischen.
5 **trolley:** Kontaktrolle (für die Oberleitung).
9 **to slink off:** sich wegschleichen, fortstehlen.
13 **snatch:** Bruchstück, Fetzen.
20 **despairingly** (adv.): verzweifelt.
21 **glimmer:** Schimmer.
23 f. **to shuffle:** schlurfen, schleifend gehen, stiefeln.

fled past me with that hasty little stride. I started and called her name. She glanced quickly over her shoulder and, seeing a man emerge from the shadow, took fright and ran. I ran too, but she put on speed and began to leave me behind. At this I despaired and shouted after her at the top of my voice.

"Kitty! Kitty! For God's sake, wait!"

She ran a few steps further and then halted incredulously. She looked back, and then turned and slowly retraced her steps.

"Jerry Moynihan!" she whispered in astonishment. "What are you doing here?"

I was summoning strength to tell her that I had happened to be taking a stroll in that direction and was surprised to see her when I realized the improbability of it and began to cry instead. Then I laughed. It was hysteria, I suppose. But Kitty had had a bad fright, and, now that she was getting over it, she was as cross as two sticks.

"Are you out of your mind or what?" she snapped.

"But I didn't see you for weeks," I said.

"What about it?" she asked. "I wasn't out."

"I thought it might be something I said to you," I said desperately.

1 **to start:** aufschrecken, zusammenzucken.
9 f. **to retrace one's steps:** denselben Weg zurückgehen.
13 **to summon strength:** Kraft aufbieten, alle Kraft zusammennehmen.
14 **stroll:** Spaziergang, Bummel.
15 **improbability:** Unwahrscheinlichkeit.
16 f. **hysteria:** Hysterie.
18 f. **as cross as two sticks:** bitterböse, stinkwütend.
20 **to snap:** barsch anfahren, schnauzen, fauchen.

"What did you say?" she asked, but I could not repeat any of the hideous things I knew I had said. I might, by accident, repeat one she hadn't noticed.

"Oh, anything," I said.

"Oh, it's not that," she said impatiently. "It's just Mother."

"Why, is there something wrong with her?" I asked almost joyously. A nice fatal or near-fatal illness might just provide me with the opportunity I needed for rushing to her rescue.

"No, but she made such a fuss of it, I felt it wasn't worth it."

"A fuss? A fuss about what?"

"About you, of course," Kitty said in exasperation.

This was worse than anything I had imagined. A woman I had never met in my life making a fuss about me. This was really terrible!

"But what did I do?" I asked.

"You didn't *do* anything, but people were talking about us just the same. And you wouldn't come in and meet her like anyone else. I know she's a bit of a fool, and her head is stuffed with old nonsense about her family. I could never see that they were different to anybody else, and anyway, she married a commercial traveller herself, so she has nothing much to talk about. Still, you needn't be so superior."

I began to shiver all over. I had thought of Kitty as a

2 **hideous:** gräßlich, abscheulich.
8 **joyously** (adv.): freudig, froh.
14 **exasperation:** Wut.
27 **to shiver:** zittern, erschauern.

secret between God, herself and me, and assumed that she only knew the half of it. Now it seemed that I didn't even know the half. People were talking about us! I was superior! What next?

"But what has she against me?" I asked, wondering if she had a spy in the office, reporting on things I said and did.

"She thinks we're doing a big tangle, of course," snapped Kitty as though she were surprised at my stupidity. "I suppose she imagines you're not grand enough for a great-great-grandniece of Daniel O'Connell. I told her you were above that sort of thing, but she wouldn't believe me. She said I was a deep, callous, crafty little intriguer and that I hadn't a drop of Daniel O'Connell's blood in my veins." Kitty giggled at the thought of herself as an intriguer, and no wonder.

"That's all she knows," I said despairingly.

"I know," Kitty agreed sadly. "The woman has no sense. And anyway she has no reason to think I'd tell her lies. Cissy and I always had fellows, and we spooned with them all over the shop under her very nose, so I don't see why she thinks I'm trying to conceal anything now."

8 **tangle:** Verstrickung, verwickelte Situation, Streit.
10 **stupidity:** Dummheit.
11 f. **O'Connell:** Daniel O'C. (1775–1847), irischer Politiker; trat für die Katholikenemanzipation und den irischen Nationalismus ein.
13 **callous:** gefühllos, hartgesotten.
14 **crafty:** listig, verschlagen.
**intriguer:** Intrigant(in).
15 **to giggle:** kichern.
20 **to spoon** (coll.): schmusen.
22 **to conceal:** verbergen.

At this I laughed like an idiot. This was worse than appalling. This was nightmare. Kitty, whom I had thought so angelic, talking in cold blood of "spooning". Even the bad women in the bad books I had read didn't talk about love-making in that cold-blooded way. Madame Bovary herself had the decency to pretend that she didn't like it. It was another door opening on an outside world, but Kitty thought I was laughing at her and began to apologize.

"Of course, I had no sense," she said. "You were the first fellow that treated me properly. The others only wanted to fool around, and now, because I don't like it, Mother is convinced I've got into something really ghastly. I can see her looking at me sideways to see is my figure all right. She really is a bit dotty. I told her I liked you better than any other fellow I knew, but that I'd grown out of that sort of thing."

"And what did she say to that?" I asked. I was beginning to see that imagination was not enough. All round me there was an objective reality that was a thousand times more nightmarish than any fantasy of my own, and I wanted to know about it, though at the same time it turned my stomach.

"Ah, I told you she was silly," Kitty said in embarrassment.

1 f. **appalling:** erschreckend, entsetzlich, abstoßend.
3 **angelic:** engelsgleich.
5 f. **Madame Bovary:** Titelheldin des gleichnamigen Romans von Gustave Flaubert (1821–80).
6 **decency:** Anstand.
14 **ghastly:** gräßlich, greulich, schauderhaft.
15 **dotty** (coll.): verrückt, bekloppt.

"Go on!" I said desperately.

"Well," said Kitty with a demure grin, "she said you were a deep, designing guttersnipe who knew exactly how to get round feather-pated little idiots like me ... I suppose I'm not clever, but I'm not as stupid as all that ... But you see, it's quite hopeless. I think she's a bit common. She doesn't understand."

"Oh, God!" I said, almost in tears. "I only wish I was."

"You wish you were what?" she asked.

"A deep, designing whatever she called me. Because then I might have some chance with you."

Kitty looked at me for a moment, and I could see she was wondering about something.

"To tell the truth, I thought you were a bit keen on me at first, but then I wasn't sure. I mean, you didn't give any indication."

"God, when I think what I've been through in the past few weeks!" I said bitterly.

"I know," said Kitty. "I was a bit fed up myself. You get used to people, I suppose."

Then we said nothing for a few moments. It didn't seem to me there was much more to be said.

"You're sure now you mean it?" she asked.

"But I tell you I was on the point of committing suicide," I said angrily.

2 **demure:** geziert, zimperlich.
3 **designing:** intrigant, ränkevoll.
**guttersnipe:** Gassenbengel.
4 **feather-pated:** hohlköpfig, töricht.
15 **to be keen on s.o.:** jdn. mögen, scharf auf jdn. sein.
20 **to be fed up:** genug, die Nase voll haben.

"Ah, what good would that be?" she asked with another shrug, and this time she looked at me and laughed outright – the little jade!

I insisted on telling her about my prospects. She didn't want to hear about my prospects; she wanted me to kiss her, but that seemed to me a very sissy sort of occupation, so I told her just the same, in the intervals. It was as if a stone had been lifted off my heart, and I went home in the moonlight, singing. Then I heard the clock strike, and the singing stopped. I remembered the mother's "Sure you won't be late?" and my own "Am I ever late?" This was desperation too, but of a different sort.

The door was ajar and the kitchen in darkness. I saw her sitting before the fire by herself, and just as I was about to throw my arms round her, I smelt Kitty's perfume and was afraid to go near her. God help us, as though that would have told her anything!

"Hullo, Mum," I said with a nervous laugh, rubbing my hands. "You're all in darkness."

"You'll have a cup of tea?" she said.

"I might as well."

"What time is it?" she said, lighting the gas. "You're very late."

"I met a fellow from the office," I said, but at the same time I was stung by the complaint in her tone.

2 **shrug:** Achselzucken.
3 **outright:** direkt, frei heraus.
**jade:** Biest, Weibsstück.
6 **sissy:** weibisch.
12 **desperation:** Verzweiflung, Hoffnungslosigkeit.
14 **ajar:** angelehnt, einen Spaltbreit offen.

"You frightened me," she said with a little whimper. "I didn't know what happened to you. What kept you at all?"

"Oh, what do you think?" I said, goaded by my own sense of guilt. "Drinking and blackguarding as usual."

I could have bitten my tongue off as I said it; it sounded so cruel, as if some stranger had said it instead of me. She turned to me with a frightened stare as if she were seeing the stranger too, and somehow I couldn't bear it.

"God Almighty!" I said. "A fellow can have no life in his own house."

I went hastily upstairs, lit the candle, undressed, and got into bed. A chap could be a drunkard and blackguard and not be made to suffer what I was being made to suffer for being out late one single night. This, I felt, was what you got for being a good son.

"Jerry," she called from the foot of the stairs, "will I bring you up your cup?"

"I don't want it now, thanks," I said.

I heard her sigh and turn away. Then she locked the doors, front and back. She didn't wash up, and I knew that my cup of tea was standing on the table with a saucer on top in case I changed my mind. She came slowly upstairs and her walk was that of an old woman. I blew out the candle before she reached the landing, in

1 **whimper:** Wimmern, Winseln.
4 **goaded:** angestachelt, getrieben.
5 **to blackguard:** Gemeinheiten begehen, sich wie ein Lump benehmen, herumpöbeln.
15 **drunkard:** Säufer.

case she came in to ask if I wanted anything else, and the moonlight came in the attic window and brought me memories of Kitty. But every time I tried to imagine her face as she grinned up at me, waiting for me to kiss her, it was the mother's face that came up instead, with that look like a child's when you strike him for the first time – as if he suddenly saw the stranger in you. I remembered all our life together from the night my father died; our early Mass on Sunday; our visits to the pictures, and our plans for the future, and Christ! it was as if I was inside her mind while she sat by the fire waiting for the blow to fall. And now it had fallen, and I was a stranger to her, and nothing I could ever do would make us the same to one another again. There was something like a cannon-ball stuck in my chest, and I lay awake till the cocks started crowing. Then I could bear it no longer. I went out on the landing and listened.

"Are you awake, Mother?" I asked in a whisper.

"What is it, Jerry?" she replied in alarm, and I knew that she hadn't slept any more than I had.

"I only came to say I was sorry," I said, opening the door of her room, and then as I saw her sitting up in bed under the Sacred Heart lamp, the cannon-ball burst inside me and I began to cry like a kid.

"Oh, child, child, child," she exclaimed; "what are you crying for at all, my little boy?" She spread out her arms to me. I went to her and she hugged me and rock-

2 **attic window:** Dach-, Mansardenfenster.
15 **cannon-ball:** Kanonenkugel.
24 **Sacred Heart:** Heiliges Herz Jesu.

ed me as she did when I was only a nipper. "Oh, oh, oh," she was saying to herself in a whisper, "my storeen bawn, my little man!" – all the names she hadn't called me in years. That was all we said. I couldn't bring myself to tell her what I had done, nor could she confess to me that she was jealous: all she could do was to try and comfort me for the way I'd hurt her, to make up to me for the nature she had given me. "My storeen bawn!" she said. "My little man!"

1 **nipper:** Dreikäsehoch, Knirps.
2 f. **my storeen bawn** (Ir.): *my darling baby.*

Doris Lessing

# Flight

Above the old man's head was the dovecote, a tall wire-netted shelf on stilts, full of strutting, preening birds. The sunlight broke on their grey breasts into small rainbows. His ears were lulled by their crooning, his hands stretched up towards his favourite, a homing pigeon, a young plump-bodied bird which stood still when it saw him and cocked a shrewd bright eye. "Pretty, pretty, pretty," he said, as he grasped the bird and drew it down, feeling the cold coral claws tighten around his finger. Content, he rested the bird lightly on his chest, and leaned against a tree, gazing out beyond the dovecote into the landscape of a late afternoon. In

3 **dovecote:** Taubenschlag.
3 f. **wire-netted:** mit Maschendraht versehen.
4 **stilt:** Stelze.
**to strut:** (herum)stolzieren.
**to preen:** sich putzen.
6 **lulled:** eingelullt, besänftigt.
**crooning:** leises Singen, Gurren.
7 f. **homing pigeon:** Brieftaube.
8 **plump-bodied:** rundlich, drall.
9 **to cock an eye:** schräg blicken, blinzeln.
**shrewd:** schlau, pfiffig.
11 **coral:** korallenrot.
**claw:** Kralle.
**to tighten:** hier: sich fest schließen.
13 **to gaze:** starren, starr blicken.

folds and hollows of sunlight and shade, the dark red soil, which was broken into great dusty clods, stretched wide to a tall horizon. Trees marked the course of the valley; a stream of rich green grass the road.

His eyes travelled homewards along this road until he saw his grand-daughter swinging on the gate underneath a frangipani tree. Her hair fell down her back in a wave of sunlight, and her long bare legs repeated the angles of the frangipani stems, bare, shining-brown stems among patterns of pale blossoms.

She was gazing past the pink flowers, past the railway cottage where they lived, along the road to the village.

His mood shifted. He deliberately held out his wrist for the bird to take flight, and caught it again at the moment it spread its wings. He felt the plump shape strive and strain under his fingers; and, in a sudden access of troubled spite, shut the bird into a small box and fastened the bolt. "Now you stay there," he muttered; and turned his back on the shelf of birds. He moved warily along the hedge, stalking his grand-daughter, who was now looped over the gate, her head loose on her arms, singing. The light happy sound mingled with the crooning of the birds, and his anger mounted.

2 **clod:** (Erd-)Klumpen, Scholle.
7 **frangipani tree:** Frangipanibaum (tropischer Zierstrauch).
17 **access:** hier: Anfall, Ausbruch.
19 **to mutter:** murmeln, brummen.
20 **warily** (adv.): argwöhnisch, vorsichtig, behutsam.
21 **to stalk s.o.:** sich an jdn. heranpirschen.
22 **looped:** gebeugt.
23 **to mingle:** sich mischen, verbinden.

"Hey!" he shouted; saw her jump, look back, and abandon the gate. Her eyes veiled themselves, and she said in a pert neutral voice: "Hullo, Grandad." Politely she moved towards him, after a lingering backward glance at the road.

"Waiting for Steven, hey?" he said, his fingers curling like claws into his palm.

"Any objection?" she asked lightly, refusing to look at him.

He confronted her, his eyes narrowed, shoulders hunched, tight in a hard knot of pain which included the preening birds, the sunlight, the flowers, herself. He said: "Think you're old enough to go courting, hey?"

The girl tossed her head at the old-fashioned phrase and sulked, "Oh, Grandad!"

"Think you want to leave home, hey? Think you can go running around the fields at night?"

Her smile made him see her, as he had every evening of this warm end-of-summer month, swinging hand in hand along the road to the village with that red-handed, red-throated, violent-bodied youth, the son of the postmaster. Misery went to his head and he shouted angrily: "I'll tell your mother!"

"Tell away!" she said, laughing, and went back to the gate.

2 **to veil o.s.:** sich verschleiern.
3 **pert:** keck, frech.
10 **to confront s.o.:** jdm. gegenübertreten.
11 **hunched:** zusammengezogen, gebeugt.
14 **to toss one's head:** den Kopf zurückwerfen.
15 **to sulk:** schmollen.
24 **tell away:** sag's nur.

He heard her singing, for him to hear:

"I've got you under my skin,
I've got you deep in the heart of . . ."

"Rubbish," he shouted. "Rubbish. Impudent little bit of rubbish!"

Growling under his breath he turned towards the dovecote, which was his refuge from the house he shared with his daughter and her husband and their children. But now the house would be empty. Gone all the young girls with their laughter and their squabbling and their teasing. He would be left, uncherished and alone, with that square-fronted, calm-eyed woman, his daughter. He stooped, muttering, before the dovecote, resenting the absorbed cooing birds.

From the gate the girl shouted: "Go and tell! Go on, what are you waiting for?"

Obstinately he made his way to the house, with quick, pathetic persistent glances of appeal back at her. But

4 **impudent:** unverschämt.
6 **to growl:** knurren, grollen.
**under one's breath:** leise, flüsternd.
7 **refuge:** Zuflucht.
10 **squabbling:** Zankerei, Kabbelei.
11 **teasing:** Neckerei.
**uncherished:** nicht liebevoll umsorgt.
12 **square-fronted:** mit eckiger Stirn, mit kantigem Gesicht.
13 **to stoop:** sich bücken, herabbeugen.
14 **absorbed:** vertieft, in Anspruch genommen.
**to coo:** gurren.
17 **obstinately** (adv.): hartnäckig, störrisch.
18 **pathetic:** pathetisch, mitleiderregend.
**persistent:** beharrlich, wiederholt.

she never looked around. Her defiant but anxious young body stung him into love and repentance. He stopped. “But I never meant. . . .” he muttered, waiting for her to turn and run to him. “I didn’t mean. . . .” She did not turn. She had forgotten him. Along the road came the young man Steven, with something in his hand. A present for her? The old man stiffened as he watched the gate swing back, and the couple embrace. In the brittle shadows of the frangipani tree his grand-daughter, his darling, lay in the arms of the postmaster’s son, and her hair flowed back over his shoulder.

“I see you!” shouted the old man spitefully. They did not move. He stumped into the little whitewashed house, hearing the wooden veranda creak angrily under his feet. His daughter was sewing in the front room, threading a needle held to the light.

He stopped again, looking back into the garden. The couple were now sauntering among the bushes, laughing. As he watched he saw the girl escape from the youth with a sudden mischievous movement, and run off through the flowers with him in pursuit. He heard shouts, laughter, a scream, silence.

1 **defiant:** trotzig, herausfordernd.
2 **repentance:** Reue.
7 **to stiffen:** erstarren, sich versteifen.
9 **brittle:** zerbrechlich, spröde, instabil.
13 **spitefully** (adv.): gehässig, hämisch.
14 **to stump:** stampfen, stapfen.
**whitewashed:** weiß getüncht.
15 **to creak:** knarren.
19 **to saunter:** schlendern.
21 **mischievous:** mutwilig, boshaft, schelmisch.

"But it's not like that at all," he muttered miserably. "It's not like that. Why can't you see? Running and giggling, and kissing and kissing. You'll come to something quite different."

He looked at his daughter with sardonic hatred, hating himself. They were caught and finished, both of them, but the girl was still running free.

"Can't you *see*?" he demanded of his invisible granddaughter, who was at that moment lying in the thick green grass with the postmaster's son.

His daughter looked at him and her eyebrows went up in tired forbearance.

"Put your birds to bed?" she asked, humouring him.

"Lucy," he said urgently. "Lucy. . . ."

"Well what is it now?"

"She's in the garden with Steven."

"Now you just sit down and have your tea."

He stumped his feet alternately, thump, thump, on the hollow wooden floor and shouted: "She'll marry him. I'm telling you, she'll be marrying him next!"

His daughter rose swiftly, brought him a cup, set him a plate.

"I don't want any tea. I don't want it, I tell you."

"Now, now," she crooned. "What's wrong with it? Why not?"

2 f. **to giggle:** kichern.
5 **sardonic:** bitter, hämisch.
8 **invisible:** unsichtbar.
12 **forbearance:** Langmut, Nachsicht.
13 **to humour s.o.:** auf jdn. eingehen, jdm. gefällig sein.
18 **alternately** (adv.): abwechselnd.
**thump:** bum!

"She's eighteen. Eighteen!"

"I was married at seventeen and I never regretted it."

"Liar," he said. "Liar. Then you should regret it. Why do you make your girls marry? It's you who do it. What do you do it for? Why?"

"The other three have done fine. They've three fine husbands. Why not Alice?"

"She's the last," he mourned. "Can't we keep her a bit longer?"

"Come, now, dad. She'll be down the road, that's all. She'll be here every day to see you."

"But it's not the same." He thought of the other three girls, transformed inside a few months from charming petulant spoiled children into serious young matrons.

"You never did like it when we married?" she said. "Why not? Every time, it's the same. When I got married you made me feel like it was something wrong. And my girls the same. You get them all crying and miserable the way you go on. Leave Alice alone. She's happy." She sighed, letting her eyes linger on the sun-lit garden. "She'll marry next month. There's no reason to wait."

"You've said they can marry?" he said incredulously.

"Yes, dad, why not?" she said coldly, and took up her sewing.

His eyes stung, and he went out on to the veranda. Wet

9 **to mourn:** klagen.
14 **transformed:** verwandelt, verändert.
15 **petulant:** launenhaft, verdrießlich, mutwillig.
**matron:** Matrone, würdige Dame.
24 **incredulously** (adv.): ungläubig.

spread down over his chin and he took out a handkerchief and mopped his whole face. The garden was empty.

From around a corner came the young couple; but their faces were no longer set against him. On the wrist of the postmaster's son balanced a young pigeon, the light gleaming on its breast.

"For me?" said the old man, letting the drops shake off his chin. "For me?"

"Do you like it?" The girl grabbed his hand and swung on it. "It's for you, Grandad. Steven brought it for you." They hung about him, affectionate, concerned, trying to charm away his wet eyes and his misery. They took his arms and directed him to the shelf of birds, one on each side, enclosing him, petting him, saying wordlessly that nothing would be changed, nothing could change, and that they would be with him always. The bird was proof of it, they said, from their lying happy eyes, as they thrust it on him. "There, Grandad, it's yours. It's for you."

They watched him as he held it on his wrist, stroking its soft, sun-warmed back, watching the wings lift and balance.

"You must shut it up for a bit," said the girl intimately. "Until it knows this is its home."

2 **to mop:** (ab)wischen.
5 **to be set against s.o.:** sich jdm. widersetzen, jdm. Widerstand zeigen.
7 **to gleam:** schimmern, leuchten, glänzen.
12 **affectionate:** liebevoll.
19 **to thrust s.th. on s.o.:** jdm. etwas aufdrängen, zuschieben.
21 **to stroke:** streicheln.
24 **intimately** (adv.): vertraulich.

"Teach your grandmother to suck eggs," growled the old man.

Released by his half-deliberate anger, they fell back, laughing at him. "We're glad you like it." They moved off, now serious and full of purpose, to the gate, where they hung, backs to him, talking quietly. More than anything could, their grown-up seriousness shut him out, making him alone; also, it quietened him, took the sting out of their tumbling like puppies on the grass. They had forgotten him again. Well, so they should, the old man reassured himself, feeling his throat clotted with tears, his lips trembling. He held the new bird to his face, for the caress of its silken feathers. Then he shut it in a box and took out his favourite.

"*Now* you can go," he said aloud. He held it poised, ready for flight, while he looked down the garden towards the boy and the girl. Then, clenched in the pain of loss, he lifted the bird on his wrist and watched it soar.

1 **Teach your grandmother to suck eggs** (prov.): etwa: Das Ei will klüger sein als die Henne.
3 **to fall back:** sich zurückziehen.
5 **full of purpose:** zielstrebig, entschlossen.
8 **to quieten:** beruhigen, besänftigen.
9 **tumbling:** Herumpurzeln, -tollen.
**puppy:** Welpe, junger Hund.
11 **to reassure:** beruhigen, versichern.
12 **clotted:** verklumpt, verdickt.
13 **caress:** Liebkosung.
**silken:** seiden, seidig.
16 **poised:** in Balance, schwebend.
18 **clenched:** angespannt, verkrampft.
19 **to soar:** aufsteigen, sich emporschwingen.

A whirr and a spatter of wings, and a cloud of birds rose into the evening from the dovecote.

At the gate Alice and Steven forgot their talk and watched the birds.

On the veranda, that woman, his daughter, stood gazing, her eyes shaded with a hand that still held her sewing.

It seemed to the old man that the whole afternoon had stilled to watch his gesture of self-command, that even the leaves of the trees had stopped shaking.

Dry-eyed and calm, he let his hands fall to his sides and stood erect, staring up into the sky.

The cloud of shining silver birds flew up and up, with a shrill cleaving of wings, over the dark ploughed land and the darker belts of trees and the bright folds of grass, until they floated high in the sunlight, like a cloud of motes of dust.

They wheeled in a wide circle, tilting their wings so there was flash after flash of light, and one after another they dropped from the sunshine of the upper sky to shadow, one after another, returning to the shadowed earth over trees and grass and field, returning to the valley and the shelter of night.

The garden was all a fluster and a flurry of returning birds. Then silence, and the sky was empty.

1 **whirr:** Schwirren.
**spatter:** Klatschen, Spritzen.
9 **self-command:** Selbstbeherrschung.
14 **cleaving:** Teilung, Trennung.
17 **mote:** Stäubchen, Teilchen.
18 **to tilt:** schräg halten, neigen.
24 **fluster:** Aufregung, Durcheinander.
**flurry:** Unruhe, Wirbel.

The old man turned, slowly, taking his time; he lifted his eyes to smile proudly down the garden at his granddaughter. She was staring at him. She did not smile. She was wide-eyed, and pale in the cold shadow, and he saw the tears run shivering off her face.

5 **to shiver:** zittern.

Ian McEwan

# First Love, Last Rites

From the beginning of summer until it seemed pointless, we lifted the thin mattress on to the heavy oak table and made love in front of the large open window. We always had a breeze blowing into the room and smells of the quayside four floors down. I was drawn into fantasies against my will, fantasies of the creature, and afterwards when we lay on our backs on the huge table, in those deep silences I heard it faintly running and clawing. It was new to me, all this, and I worried, I tried to talk to Sissel about it for reassurance. She had nothing to say, she did not make abstractions or discuss situations, she lived inside them. We watched the seagulls wheeling about in our square of sky and wondered if they had been watching us up there, that was the kind of thing we talked about, mildly entertaining

2 **last rites:** Sterbesakramente (*rite:* Ritus, Zeremoniell, feierlicher Brauch).
3 f. **pointless:** sinn-, zwecklos.
4 **mattress:** Matratze.
6 **breeze:** Brise, leichter Wind.
7 **quayside:** Kaistraße, -gelände, -anlage.
8 **fantasy:** Phantasie(vorstellung).
11 **to claw:** kratzen, schrammen, scharren.
12 **reassurance:** Beruhigung, Ermutigung, Versicherung.
13 **abstraction:** Abstraktion, abstrakter Begriff, Theorie.
15 **seagull:** Möwe.

hypotheses of the present moment. Sissel did things as they came to her, stirred her coffee, made love, listened to her records, looked out the window. She did not say things like I'm happy, or confused, or I want to make love, or I don't, or I'm tired of the fights in my family, she had no language to split herself in two, so I suffered alone what seemed like crimes in my head while we fucked, and afterwards listened alone to it scrabbling in the silence. Then one afternoon Sissel woke from a doze, raised her head from the mattress and said, "What's that scratching noise behind the wall?"

My friends were far away in London, they sent me anguished and reflective letters, what would they do now? Who were they, and what was the point of it all? They were my age, seventeen and eighteen, but I pretended not to understand them. I sent back postcards, find a big table and an open window, I told them. I was happy and it seemed easy, I was making eel traps, it was so easy to have a purpose. The summer went on and I no longer heard from them. Only Adrian came to see us, he was Sissel's ten-year-old brother and he came to escape the misery of his disintegrating home, the quick reversals of his mother's moods, the endless competi-

1 **hypothesis** (pl. *hypotheses*): Hypothese, Vermutung.
8 **to fuck** (vulg.): ficken, vögeln.
**to scrabble:** scharren, kratzen.
10 **doze:** Schläfchen, Nickerchen.
12 f. **anguished:** gequält, gepeinigt, angstvoll, schmerzvoll.
13 **reflective:** nachdenklich.
18 **eel:** Aal.
**trap:** Reuse.
22 **to disintegrate:** sich auflösen; auseinanderfallen, -brechen.
23 **reversal:** Umschlag, Umschwung.

tive piano playing of his sisters, the occasional bitter visits of his father. Adrian and Sissel's parents after twenty-seven years of marriage and six children hated each other with sour resignation, they could no longer bear to live in the same house. The father moved out to a hostel a few streets away to be near his children. He was a businessman who was out of work and looked like Gregory Peck, he was an optimist and had a hundred schemes to make money in an interesting way. I used to meet him in the pub. He did not want to talk about his redundancy or his marriage, he did not mind me living in a room over the quayside with his daughter. Instead he told me about his time in the Korean war, and when he was an international salesman, and of the legal fraudery of his friends who were now at the top and knighted, and then one day of the eels in the River Ouse, how the river bed swarmed with eels, how there was money to be made catching them and taking them alive to London. I told him how I had eighty pounds in the bank, and the next morning we bought netting, twine, wire hoops and an old cistern tank to keep eels in. I spent the next two months making eel traps.

6 **hostel:** Herberge, Männerheim.
11 **redundancy:** Entlassung, Erwerbslosigkeit.
13 f. **Korean war:** Koreakrieg (1950–53).
15 **fraudery:** Betrügerei, Schwindelei, Gaunerei.
16 **to knight:** zum Ritter schlagen, in den Adelsstand erheben.
17 **to swarm:** wimmeln.
21 **netting:** Netz(werk).
**twine:** (Bind-)Faden, Schnur.
**hoop:** Reifen.
**cistern tank:** Wasserbehälter.

On fine days I took my net, hoops and twine outside and worked on the quay, sitting on a bollard. An eel trap is cylinder-shaped, sealed at one end, and at the other is a long tapering funnel entrance. It lies on the river bed, the eels swim in to eat the bait and in their blindness cannot find their way out. The fishermen were friendly and amused. There's eels down there, they said, and you'll catch a few but you won't make no living on it. The tide'll lose your nets fast as you make them. We're using iron weights, I told them, and they shrugged in a good-natured way and showed me a better way to lash the net to the hoops, they believed it was my right to try it for myself. When the fishermen were out in their boats and I did not feel like working I sat about and watched the tidal water slip across the mud, I felt no urgency about the eel traps but I was certain we would be rich.

I tried to interest Sissel in the eel adventure, I told her about the rowing-boat someone was lending to us for the summer, but she had nothing to say. So instead we lifted the mattress on to the table and lay down with our clothes on. Then she began to talk. We pressed our

2 **quay:** Kai, Uferstraße.
**bollard:** (Beleg-)Poller (Holz- oder Metallpfosten zum Befestigen der Taue).
3 **cylinder-shaped:** zylindrisch.
4 **to taper:** spitz zulaufen, sich verjüngen.
**funnel:** Trichter.
5 **bait:** Köder.
11 **to shrug:** die Achseln zucken.
**good-natured:** gutmütig.
12 **to lash:** festzurren, anbinden.
15 **tidal water:** Flutwasser.

palms together, she made a careful examination of the size and shape of our hands and gave a running commentary. Exactly the same size, your fingers are thicker, you've got this extra bit here. She measured my eye-lashes with the end of her thumb and wished hers were as long, she told me about the dog she had when she was small, it had long white eye-lashes. She looked at the sunburn on my nose and talked about that, which of her brothers and sisters went red in the sun, who went brown, what her youngest sister said once. We slowly undressed. She kicked off her plimsolls and talked about her foot rot. I listened with my eyes closed, I could smell mud and seaweed and dust through the open window. Wittering on, she called it, this kind of talk. Then once I was inside her I was moved, I was inside my fantasy, there could be no separation now of my mushrooming sensations from my knowledge that we could make a creature grow in Sissel's belly. I had no wish to be a father, that was not in it at all. It was eggs, sperms, chromosomes, feathers, gills, claws,

2 **running:** fortlaufend.
2 f. **commentary:** Kommentar, Erläuterungen.
4 f. **eyelash:** Wimper.
8 **sunburn:** Sonnenbrand.
11 **to kick off:** wegschleudern, abschütteln.
**plimsolls:** Turnschuhe.
12 **foot rot:** Fußpilz.
13 **seaweed:** Seetang, Meeresalge.
14 **to witter on:** vor sich hin labern, plappern.
17 **to mushroom:** wild wachsen, wuchern.
20 **sperm:** Sperma, Same(n).
**chromosome:** Chromosom, Kernstäbchen.
**gill:** Kiemen.
**claw:** Klaue, Kralle.

inches from my cock's end the unstoppable chemistry of a creature growing out of a dark red slime, my fantasy was of being helpless before the age and strength of this process and the thought alone could make me come before I wanted. When I told Sissel she laughed. Oh, Gawd, she said. To me Sissel was right inside the process, she *was* the process and the power of its fascination grew. She was meant to be on the pill and every month she forgot it at least two or three times. Without discussion we came to the arrangement that I was to come outside her, but it rarely worked. As we were swept down the long slopes to our orgasms, in those last desperate seconds I struggled to find my way out but I was caught like an eel in my fantasy of the creature in the dark, waiting, hungry, and I fed it great white gobs. In those careless fractions of a second I abandoned my life to feeding the creature, whatever it was, in or out of the womb, to fucking only Sissel, to feeding more creatures, my whole life given over to this in a moment's weakness. I watched out for Sissel's periods, everything about women was new to me and I could take nothing for granted. We made love in Sis-

1 **cock** (slang): Pimmel, Penis.
**unstoppable:** unaufhaltsam.
2 **slime:** Schleim.
6 **Gawd:** *God.*
8 **to be on the pill:** die (Anti-Baby-)Pille nehmen.
12 **orgasm:** Orgasmus, Höhepunkt.
16 **gob:** Schleimklumpen, Auswurf, Qualster.
18 **womb:** Schoß, Mutterleib, Gebärmutter.
21 **period:** (Menstruations-)Periode, Regel.
22 **to take s.th. for granted:** etwas als selbstverständlich annehmen.

sel's copious, effortless periods, got good and sticky and brown with the blood and I thought we were the creatures now in the slime, we were inside fed by gobs of cloud coming through the window, by gases drawn from the mudflats by the sun. I worried about my fantasies, I knew I could not come without them. I asked Sissel what she thought about and she giggled. Not feathers and gills, anyway. What *do* you think about, then? Nothing much, nothing really. I pressed my question and she withdrew into silence.

I knew it was my own creature I heard scrabbling, and when Sissel heard it one afternoon and began to worry, I realized her fantasies were involved too, it was a sound which grew out of our lovemaking. We heard it when we were finished and lying quite still on our backs, when we were empty and clear, perfectly quiet. It was the impression of small claws scratching blindly against a wall, such a distant sound it needed two people to hear it. We thought it came from one part of thc wall. When I knelt down and put my ear to the skirting-board it stopped, I sensed it on the other side of the wall, frozen in its action, waiting in the dark. As the weeks passed we heard it at other times in the day, and now and then at night. I wanted to ask Adrian what he thought it was. Listen, there it is, Adrian, shut up a

1 **copious:** üppig, reichlich, ausgiebig.
**effortless:** mühelos, leicht.
5 **mudflat:** Schlammzone, Schlickstrecke.
7 **to giggle:** kichern.
9 **to press s.th.:** auf etwas bestehen.
14 **lovemaking:** Beischlaf, Geschlechtsverkehr.
21 **skirting-board:** Fußleiste, Scheuerleiste.

moment, what do you think that noise is, Adrian? He strained impatiently to hear what we could hear but he would not be still long enough. There's nothing there, he shouted. Nothing, nothing, nothing. He became very excited, jumped on his sister's back, yelling and yodelling. He did not want whatever it was to be heard, he did not want to be left out. I pulled him off Sissel's back and we rolled about on the bed. Listen again, I said, pinning him down, there it was again. He struggled free and ran out of the room shouting his two-tone police-car siren. We listened to it fade down the stairs and when I could hear him no more I said, Perhaps Adrian is really afraid of mice. Rats, you mean, said his sister, and put her hands between my legs.

By mid-July we were not so happy in our room, there was a growing dishevelment and unease, and it did not seem possible to discuss it with Sissel. Adrian was coming to us every day now because it was the summer holidays and he could not bear to be at home. We would hear him four floors down, shouting and stamping on the stairs on his way up to us. He came in noisily, doing handstands and showing off to us. Frequently he jumped on Sissel's back to impress me, he was anxious, he was worried we might not find him good company and send him away, send him back home. He was worried too because he could no longer understand his sis-

5 f. **to yodel:** jodeln.
9 **to pin s.o. down:** jdn. festhalten, festnageln.
11 **siren:** Sirene.
16 **dishevelment:** Ungepflegtheit, Schlampigkeit, Wirrheit.
**unease:** Unbehagen, Unruhe.
22 **to show off:** angeben, prahlen; sich produzieren.

ter. At one time she was always ready for a fight, and she was a good fighter, I heard him boast that to his friends, he was proud of her. Now changes had come over his sister, she pushed him off sulkily, she wanted to be left alone to do nothing, she wanted to listen to records. She was angry when he got his shoes on her skirt, and she had breasts now like his mother, she talked to him now like his mother. Get down off there, Adrian. Please, Adrian, please, not now, later. He could not quite believe it all the same, it was a mood of his sister's, a phase, and he went on taunting and attacking her hopefully, he badly wanted things to stay as they were before his father left home. When he locked his forearms round Sissel's neck and pulled her backwards on to the bed his eyes were on me for encouragement, he thought the real bond was between us, the two men against the girl. He did not see there was no encouragement, he wanted it so badly. Sissel never sent Adrian away, she understood why he was here, but it was hard for her. One long afternoon of torment she left the room almost crying with frustration. Adrian turned to me and raised his eyebrows in mock horror. I tried to talk to him then but he was already making his yodelling sound and squaring up for a fight with me. Nor did Sissel have anything to say to me about her brother, she never made general remarks about people because

4 **sulkily** (adv.): mürrisch, verdrießlich, verdrossen, schmollend.
11 **to taunt:** sticheln, verspotten, reizen.
20 **torment:** Folter, Qual, Pein.
22 **mock:** gespielt, Schein-.
24 **to square up:** sich vor jdm. aufbauen, aufpflanzen; in Kampfstellung gehen.

she never made general remarks. Sometimes when we heard Adrian on his way up the stairs she glanced across at me and seemed to betray herself by a slight pursing of her beautiful lips.

There was only one way to persuade Adrian to leave us in peace. He could not bear to see us touch, it pained him, it genuinely disgusted him. When he saw one of us move across the room to the other he pleaded with us silently, he ran between us, pretending playfulness, wanted to decoy us into another game. He imitated us frantically in a desperate last attempt to show us how fatuous we appeared. Then he could stand it no more, he ran out of the room machine-gunning German soldiers and young lovers on the stairs.

But Sissel and I were touching less and less now, in our quiet ways we could not bring ourselves to it. It was not that we were in decline, not that we did not delight in each other, but that our opportunities were faded. It was the room itself. It was no longer four floors up and detached, there was no breeze through the windows, only a mushy heat rising off the quayside and dead jellyfish and clouds of flies, fiery grey flies who found our

3 **to betray:** verraten.
4 **to purse one's lips:** die Lippen schürzen.
7 **to disgust:** abstoßen, ekeln.
9 **playfulness:** Ausgelassenheit, Munterkeit, Verspieltheit, Spaß.
10 **to decoy s.o. into s.th.:** jdn. in etwas locken.
11 **frantically** (adv.): stürmisch, wie wild.
12 **fatuous:** dumm, einfältig, albern.
13 **to machine-gun:** (mit einem MG) niedermähen.
19 f. **detached:** abgetrennt, abgesondert.
21 **mushy:** breiig, breiartig, weich.
21 f. **jellyfish:** Qualle.
22 **fiery:** feurig, hitzig.

armpits and bit fiercely, houseflies who hung in clouds over our food. Our hair was too long and dank and hung in our eyes. The food we bought melted and tasted like the river. We no longer lifted the mattress on to the table, the coolest place now was the floor and the floor was covered with greasy sand which would not go away. Sissel grew tired of her records, and her foot rot spread from one foot to the other and added to the smell. Our room stank. We did not talk about leaving because we did not talk about anything. Every night now we were woken by the scrabbling behind the wall, louder now and more insistent. When we made love it listened to us behind the wall. We made love less and our rubbish gathered around us, milk bottles we could not bring ourselves to carry away, grey sweating cheese, butter wrappers, yogurt cartons, over-ripe salami. And among it all Adrian cartwheeling, yodelling, machine-gunning and attacking Sissel. I tried to write poems about my fantasies, about the creature, but I could see no way in and I wrote nothing down, not even a first line. Instead I took long walks along the river dyke into the Norfolk hinterland of dull beet fields, telegraph poles, uniform grey skies. I had two more eel nets to

1 **armpit:** Achselhöhle.
2 **dank:** klamm, feucht, dumpfig, naßkalt.
6 **greasy:** fettig, schmierig.
12 **insistent:** nachdrücklich, beharrlich.
16 **wrapper:** (Einwickel-)Papier.
**carton:** Becher.
17 **to cartwheel:** radschlagen.
21 **dyke:** Deich.
22 **beet:** Runkel-, Zuckerrübe.
23 **uniform:** gleichförmig.

make, I was forcing myself to sit down to them each day. But in my heart I was sick of them, I could not really believe that eels would ever go inside them and I wondered if I wanted them to, if it was not better that the eels should remain undisturbed in the cool mud at the bottom of the river. But I went on with it because Sissel's father was ready to begin, because I had to expiate all the money and hours I had spent so far, because the idea had its own tired, fragile momentum now and I could no more stop it than carry the milk bottles from our room.

Then Sissel found a job and it made me see we were different from no one, they all had rooms, houses, jobs, careers, that's what they all did, they had cleaner rooms, better jobs, we were anywhere's striving couple. It was one of the windowless factories across the river where they canned vegetables and fruit. For ten hours a day she was to sit in the roar of machines by a moving conveyor belt, talk to no one and pick out the rotten carrots before they were canned. At the end of her first day Sissel came home in a pink-and-white nylon raincoat and pink cap. I said, Why don't you take it off? Sissel shrugged. It was all the same to her, sitting around in the room, sitting around in a factory where they relayed Radio One through speakers strung along

8 **to expiate:** abbüßen, sühnen, wiedergutmachen.
9 **fragile:** zerbrechlich.
**momentum:** Trieb-, Stoßkraft; Schwung; Eigengesetzlichkeit.
17 **to can:** in Büchsen einlegen, konservieren.
19 **conveyor belt:** Fließband.
25 **to relay:** übertragen, ausstrahlen.

the steel girders, where four hundred women half listened, half dreamed, while their hands spun backwards and forwards like powered shuttles. On Sissel's second day I took the ferry across the river and waited for her at the factory gates. A few women stepped through a small tin door in a great windowless wall and a wailing siren sounded all across the factory complex. Other small doors opened and they streamed out, converging on the gates, scores of women in pink-and-white nylon coats and pink caps. I stood on a low wall and tried to see Sissel, it was suddenly very important. I thought that if I could not pick her out from this rustling stream of pink nylon then she was lost, we were both lost and our time was worthless. As it approached the factory gates the main body was moving fast. Some were half running in the splayed, hopeless way that women have been taught to run, the others walked as fast as they could. I found out later they were hurrying home to cook suppers for their families, to make an early start on the housework. Latecomers on the next shift tried to push their way through in the opposite direction. I could not see Sissel and I felt on the edge of panic, I shouted her name and my words were trampled under-

1 **girder:** Träger.
3 **powered:** angetrieben, mechanisch.
**shuttle:** (Weber-)Schiffchen.
4 **ferry:** Fähre.
6 **to wail:** plärren, heulen, klagen.
8 **to converge:** zusammenströmen, -laufen.
12 **to rustle:** rascheln.
16 **splayed:** spreizfüßig, gespreizt, auswärts gebogen.
23 f. **underfoot:** mit dem Fuß, auf dem Boden.

foot. Two older women who stopped by the wall to light cigarettes grinned up at me. Sizzle yerself. I walked home by the long way, over the bridge, and decided not to tell Sissel I had been to wait for her because I would have to explain my panic and I did not know how. She was sitting on the bed when I came in, she was still wearing her nylon coat. The cap was on the floor. Why don't you take that thing off? I said. She said, Was that you outside the factory? I nodded. Why didn't you speak to me if you saw me standing there? Sissel turned and lay face downwards on the bed. Her coat was stained and smelled of machine oil and earth. I dunno, she said into the pillow, I didn't think. I didn't think of anything after my shift. Her words had a deadening finality, I glanced around our room and fell silent.

Two days later, on Saturday afternoon, I bought pounds of rubbery cows' lungs sodden with blood (lights, they were called) for bait. That same afternoon we filled the traps and rowed out into mid-channel at low tide to lay them on the river bed. Each of the seven traps was marked by a buoy. Four o'clock Sunday morning Sissel's father called for me and we set out in

2 **to sizzle:** brutzeln, zischen (Wortspiel mit dem Namen Sissel).
**yerself:** *yourself.*
13 **dunno:** *don't know.*
15 **to deaden:** abtöten, abstumpfen.
**finality:** Endgültigkeit.
18 **rubbery:** gummiartig.
**sodden:** aufgedunsen, aufgeschwemmt; durchweicht, klitschig.
19 **lights** (pl.): Beuschel (Lungengericht).
20 **mid-channel:** Mitte des Flußbetts, der Stromrinne.
22 **buoy:** Boje.

his van to where we kept the borrowed boat. We were rowing out now to find the marker buoys and pull the traps in, it was the testing time, would there be eels in the nets, would it be profitable to make more nets, catch more eels and drive them once a week to Billingsgate market, would we be rich? It was a dull windy morning. I felt no anticipation, only tiredness and a continuous erection. I half dozed in the warmth of the van's heater. I had spent many hours of the night awake listening to the scrabbling noises behind the wall. Once I got out of bed and banged the skirting-board with a spoon. There was a pause, then the digging continued. It seemed certain now that it was digging its way into the room. While Sissel's father rowed I watched over the side for markers. It was not as easy as I thought to find them, they did not show up white against the water but as dark low silhouettes. It was twenty minutes before we found the first. As we pulled it up I was amazed at how soon the clean white rope from the chandlers had become like all other ropes near the river, brown and hung about with fine strands of green weed. The net too was old-looking and alien, I could not believe that one of us had made it. Inside were two crabs and a large eel. He untied the closed end of the

2 **marker:** Markier-, Markierung.
5 f. **Billingsgate market:** Fischmarkt in London.
8 **to doze:** dösen.
11 **to bang:** schlagen, klopfen.
20 **chandler:** Krämer, Händler.
21 **strand:** Strähne, Strang, Flechte.
22 **alien:** fremd(artig).
24 **crab:** Taschenkrebs.

trap, let the two crabs drop into the water and put the eel in the plastic bucket we had brought with us. We put fresh lights in the trap and dropped it over the side. It took another fifteen minutes to find the next trap and that one had nothing inside. We rowed up and down the channel for half an hour after that without finding another trap, and by this time the tide was coming up and covering the markers. It was then that I took the oars and made for the shore.

We went back to the hostel where Sissel's father was staying and he cooked breakfast. We did not want to discuss the lost traps, we pretended to ourselves and to each other that we would find them when we went out at the next low tide. But we knew they were lost, swept up or downstream by the powerful tides, and I knew I could never make another eel trap in my life. I knew also that my partner was taking Adrian with him on a short holiday, they were leaving that afternoon. They were going to visit military airfields, and hoped to end up at the Imperial War Museum. We ate eggs, bacon and mushrooms and drank coffee. Sissel's father told me of an idea he had, a simple but lucrative idea. Shrimps cost very little on the quayside here and they were very expensive in Brussels. We could drive two vanloads across there each week, he was optimistic in

9 **oar:** Ruder.
15 **up or downstream:** flußauf- oder -abwärts.
19 **airfield:** Flugplatz, Flugfeld.
20 **Imperial War Museum:** Londoner Museum mit Exponaten zu den beiden Weltkriegen.
22 **lucrative:** lukrativ, einträglich.
23 **shrimp:** Krabbe.

his relaxed, friendly way and for a moment I was sure his scheme would work. I drank the last of my coffee. Well, I said, I suppose that needs some thinking about. I picked up the bucket with the eel in, Sissel and I could eat that one. My partner told me as we shook hands that the surest way of killing an eel was to cover it with salt. I wished him a good holiday and we parted, still maintaining the silent pretence that one of us would be rowing out at the next low tide to search for the traps.

After a week at the factory I did not expect Sissel to be awake when I got home, but she was sitting up in bed, pale and clasping her knees. She was staring into one corner of the room. It's in here, she said. It's behind those books on the floor. I sat down on the bed and took off my wet shoes and socks. The mouse? You mean you heard the mouse? Sissel spoke quietly. It's a rat. I saw it run across the room, and it's a rat. I went over to the books and kicked them, and instantly it was out, I heard its claws on the floorboards and then I saw it run along the wall, the size of a small dog it seemed to me then, a rat, a squat, powerful grey rat dragging its belly along the floor. It ran the whole length of the wall and crept behind a chest of drawers. We've got to get it out of here, Sissel wailed, in a voice which was strange to me. I nodded, but I could not move for the moment, or speak, it was so big, the rat, and it had been with us

13 **to clasp:** umfassen, -klammern.
20 **floorboard:** Dielenbrett.
22 **squat:** gedrungen, untersetzt.
24 **chest of drawers:** Kommode.

all summer, scrabbling at the wall in the deep, clear silences after our fucking, and in our sleep, it was our familiar. I was terrified, more afraid than Sissel, I was certain the rat knew us as well as we knew it, it was aware of us in the room now just as we were aware of it behind the chest of drawers. Sissel was about to speak again when we heard a noise on the stairs, a familiar stamping, machine-gunning noise. I was relieved to hear it. Adrian came in the way he usually did, he kicked the door and leaped in, crouching low, a machine-gun ready at his hip. He sprayed us with raw noises from the back of his throat, we crossed our lips with our fingers and tried to hush him. You're dead, both of you, he said, and got ready for a cartwheel across the room. Sissel shushed him again, she tried to wave him towards the bed. Why sshh? What's wrong with you? We pointed to the chest of drawers. It's a rat, we told him. He was down on his knees at once, peering. A rat? he gasped. Fantastic, it's a big one, look at it. Fantastic. What are you going to do? Let's catch it. I crossed the room quickly and picked up a poker from the fireplace, I could lose my fear in Adrian's excitement, pretend it

2 f. **familiar:** Vertraute(r), intime(r) Bekannte(r).
3 **terrified:** voller Angst.
10 **to crouch:** gebückt gehen, kriechen.
11 **to spray:** hier: durchsieben, durchgarben.
13 **to hush s.o.:** jdn. zum Schweigen bringen.
14 **cartwheel:** Rad(schlag).
15 **to shush:** zum Schweigen bringen, Ruhe gebieten.
16 **sshh:** sch, pst.
18 **to peer:** spähen.
**to gasp:** keuchen.
21 **poker:** Schüreisen, Feuerhaken.

was just a fat rat in our room, an adventure to catch it. From the bed Sissel wailed again. What are you going to do with that? For a moment I felt my grip loosen on the poker, it was not just a rat, it was not an adventure, we both knew that. Meanwhile Adrian danced his dance. Yes, that, use that. Adrian helped me carry the books across the room, we built a wall right round the chest of drawers with only one gap in the middle where the rat could get through. Sissel went on asking, What are you doing? What are you going to do with that? but she did not dare leave the bed. We had finished the wall and I was giving Adrian a coat-hanger to drive the rat out with when Sissel jumped across the room and tried so snatch the poker from my hand. Give me that, she cried, and hung on to my lifted arm. At that moment the rat ran out through the gap in the books, it ran straight at us and I thought I saw its teeth bared and ready. We scattered, Adrian jumped on the table, Sissel and I were back on the bed. Now we all had time to see the rat as it paused in the centre of the room and then ran forward again, we had time to see how powerful and fat and fast it was, how its whole body quivered, how its tail slid behind it like an attendant parasite. It knows us, I thought, it wants us. I could not bring myself to look at Sissel. As I stood up on the bed, raised the poker and aimed it, she screamed. I threw it as hard

12 **coat-hanger:** Kleiderbügel.
14 **to snatch:** (weg)schnappen, entreißen.
17 **to bare one's teeth:** die Zähne fletschen, blecken, entblößen.
22 **to quiver:** zittern, beben.
23 **attendant:** begleitend.
**parasite:** Parasit, Schmarotzer.

as I could, it struck the floor point first several inches from the rat's narrow head. It turned instantly and ran back between the gap in the books. We heard the scratch of its claws on the floor as it settled itself behind the chest of drawers to wait.

I unwound the wire coat-hanger, straightened it and doubled it over and gave it to Adrian. He was quieter now, slightly more fearful. His sister sat on the bed with her knees drawn up again. I stood several feet from the gap in the books with the poker held tight in both hands. I glanced down and saw my pale bare feet and saw a ghost rat's teeth bared and tearing nail from flesh. I called out, Wait, I want to get my shoes. But it was too late, Adrian was jabbing the wire behind the chest of drawers and now I dared not move. I crouched a little lower over the poker, like a batsman. Adrian climbed on to the chest and thrust the wire right down into the corner. He was in the middle of shouting something to me, I did not hear what it was. The frenzied rat was running through the gap, it was running at my feet to take its revenge. Like the ghost rat its teeth were bared. With both hands I swung the poker down, caught it clean and whole smack under its belly, and it lifted clear off the ground, sailed across the room, borne up by Sissel's long scream through her hand in her mouth, it dashed against the wall and I thought in

4 **scratch:** Gekratze, Gescharre, Scharren.
7 **to double s.th. over:** etwas zusammenbiegen.
14 **to jab:** stechen, stoßen, stochern.
16 **batsman:** Schlagmann beim Kricket.
19 **frenzied:** rasend, toll, wahnsinnig.
23 **smack** (adv.): klatsch; direkt, voll, ganz.

an instant, it must have broken its back. It dropped to the ground, legs in the air, split from end to end like a ripe fruit. Sissel did not take her hand from her mouth, Adrian did not move from the chest, I did not shift my weight from where I had struck, and no one breathed out. A faint smell crept across the room, musty and intimate, like the smell of Sissel's monthly blood. Then Adrian farted and giggled from his held-back fear, his human smell mingled with the wide-open rat smell. I stood over the rat and prodded it gently with the poker. It rolled on its side, and from the mighty gash which ran its belly's length there obtruded and slid partially free from the lower abdomen a translucent purple bag, and inside five pale crouching shapes, their knees drawn up around their chins. As the bag touched the floor I saw a movement, the leg of one unborn rat quivered as if in hope, but the mother was hopelessly dead and there was no more for it.

Sissel knelt by the rat, Adrian and I stood behind her like guards, it was as if she had some special right, kneeling there with her long red skirt spilling round her. She parted the gash in the mother rat with her forefinger and thumb, pushed the bag back inside and

6 **musty:** modrig, muffig, dumpfig.
8 **to fart:** furzen, pupsen.
10 **to prod:** anstoßen, stochern.
11 **gash:** klaffende Wunde, Spalt, Schlitz, Riß.
12 **to obtrude:** herausdrängen, -hängen.
13 **lower abdomen:** Unterleib.
**translucent:** durchsichtig.
**purple:** purpurrot.
21 **to spill:** sich ergießen.

closed the blood-spiked fur over it. She remained kneeling a little while and we still stood behind her. Then she cleared some dishes from the sink to wash her hands. We all wanted to get outside now, so Sissel wrapped the rat in newspaper and we carried it downstairs. Sissel lifted the lid of the dustbin and I placed it carefully inside. Then I remembered something, I told the other two to wait for me and I ran back up the stairs. It was the eel I came back for, it lay quite still in its few inches of water and for a moment I thought that it too was dead till I saw it stir when I picked up the bucket. The wind had dropped now and the cloud was breaking up, we walked to the quay in alternative light and shade. The tide was coming in fast. We walked down the stone steps to the water's edge and there I tipped the eel back in the river and we watched him flick out of sight, a flash of white underside in the brown water. Adrian said goodbye to us, and I thought he was going to hug his sister. He hesitated and then ran off, calling out something over his shoulder. We shouted after him to have a good holiday. On the way back Sissel and I stopped to look at the factories on the other side of the river. She told me she was going to give up her job there.

We lifted the mattress on to the table and lay down in front of the open window, face to face, the way we did at the beginning of summer. We had a light breeze

1 **blood-spiked:** mit Stacheln aus (geronnenem) Blut.
6 **dustbin:** Mülltonne.
17 **to flick:** (davon)schnellen.
**underside:** Unterseite, Unterleib; Bauch.

blowing in, a distant smoky smell of autumn, and I felt calm, very clear. Sissel said, This afternoon let's clean the room up and then go for a long walk, a walk along the river dyke. I pressed the flat of my palm against her warm belly and said, Yes.

Penelope Lively

# The Art of Biography

She was eighty if she was a day. Which was of course to be expected: Edward Lamprey would be eighty-seven if he were still alive and the daughter had said Miss Rockingham was a contemporary. Miss Lucinda Rockingham. A curiously lavish name for the spare, slightly bent old lady who stood now in her doorway, looking up at him.

He put out a hand, smiled his charming open young man's smile. "Miss Rockingham? I'm Malcolm Sanders. It's so good of you to let me take up your time like this."

Twenty-eight interviews, duly recorded and filed. Seventeen card index boxes. Seven hundred and nineteen letters in the British Library and the University of Texas and in God knows how many box files and drawers of desks. Notes and footnotes and references and cross-references; checks and cross-checks and headings and sub-headings. Names and places and times and dates.

3 **eighty if she was a day:** mindestens achtzig.
7 **lavish:** üppig, aufwendig.
**spare:** schlank.
14 **duly** (adv.): ordnungsgemäß.
15 **card index box:** Karteikasten.
18 **footnote:** Fußnote.
18 f. **cross-reference:** Querverweis.
20 **sub-heading:** Untertitel.

All sewn up and stashed away, or just about. A man's life reduced to paper and print – or rather, card and tempo pen. The material, the valuable laboriously gathered material for the definitive biography of Edward Lamprey, poet and man of letters, born eighteen-ninety-three, died nineteen-fifty-eight.

He yawned, discreetly, into the back of his hand, turning momentarily aside as though to admire the view of the estuary beyond the wide window of Lucinda Rockingham's sitting-room. A flat, melancholy East Anglian view, all sea and sky and fleeing birds and, far away, cars twinkling along the coast road. Bleak and impersonal, as was the house bleak and impersonal – an Edwardian villa, faintly hostile from without and chilly within, the sofa too hard, the room too neat, the pictures too square upon the walls.

And Lucinda Rockingham an agreeable enough old thing but not of any use, he could tell within the first five minutes, nothing of any significance to say about

1 **to stash away:** horten, sicher verwahren.
3 **laboriously** (adv.): mühsam, fleißig.
5 **man of letters:** Literat, Gelehrter.
7 **discreetly** (adv.): diskret, unauffällig.
9 **estuary:** Meeresbucht.
10 **melancholy:** melancholisch.
10 f. **East Anglian:** Adjektiv zu *East Anglia*; zu dem angelsächsischen Königreich, heute größtenteils Gebiet der Grafschaften Norfolk und Suffolk im Osten Englands, gehörend.
12 **to twinkle:** glitzern, funkeln.
**bleak:** öde, kahl.
13 **impersonal:** unpersönlich.
14 **Edwardian:** aus der Zeit Edwards VII. (frühes 20. Jh.).
15 **chilly:** kühl, frostig.
17 **agreeable:** angenehm, liebenswürdig.

Lamprey ("He was a great poet, you know, Mr Sanders, yes, I knew him since nineteen-forty, yes, he visited this house ..."), the trip a waste.

He smiled and jotted the odd note and let his mind drift. He examined his feelings – took them out and prodded them, held them up to the light, took their temperature, and they were the same. He was in love, no two ways about it. Conjure her up, right here on the worn patterned carpet beside the unlit Rayburn Maxistove, and there was that delicious liquefaction of the vitals. He smiled and made another note and held her in his arms, against his cheek, her mouth ... Better phone as soon as he was through here, before she left the office, there was a phone booth on the sea-front, he'd just catch her if he cut this short ...

That, actually, was the funny thing about Lamprey. The one odd, unsatisfactory blank. Love. For a man whose passionate nature spun from every line of the poems, the absence of any evidence that he ever experienced intensity of love was curious to say the least of it. Certainly there'd been none in the marriage, probably not

4 **to jot:** notieren, flüchtig vermerken.
5 **to drift:** (dahin)treiben, wandern.
6 **to prod:** anstupsen, -stechen.
8 **no two ways about it:** ohne Zweifel; etwas anderes kam nicht in Frage.
**to conjure s.th. up:** etwas hervor-, herbeizaubern, beschwören.
9 f. **Rayburn Maxistove:** Holz-, Kohleofen (Markenname).
10 **liquefaction:** Verflüssigung, Schmelzung.
11 **vitals:** lebenswichtige Organe; edle Körperteile.
14 **phone booth:** Telefonzelle.
20 **intensity:** Intensität.

even at the very beginning. A haphazard union that drifted into a convenient arrangement for the upbringing of the four cherished daughters. For them, certainly, there had been love, devotion indeed, but not the kind of love to account for the depth of feeling that lurked in the poetry, the pastoral poems in particular that read at times like something quite other, like . . .

". . . occasionally helped with some of the more tedious clerical tasks," said the old lady. "The study of Coleridge, which I daresay you know . . ." She smoothed the cotton print dress across her knees and smiled, a rather sweet smile, a beauty once probably – no, not a beauty, just a very pretty woman (no husband, apparently, odd, that) – and bless her yes one did indeed know the study of Coleridge, every chapter and verse of it, what did she imagine one had spent three years doing, for heaven's sake? The daughters had had some vague idea that she did odd bits of secretarial stuff for Lamprey, that sort of thing – the kind of useful friend a man like that sometimes attracts. But they'd not known much about her, none of them, only as a name that cropped up once or twice, hadn't suggested her until this late point, with

1 **haphazard:** willkürlich, zufällig.
2 f. **upbringing:** Erziehung.
3 **cherished:** zärtlich geliebt, verehrt.
6 **to lurk:** lauern, verborgen liegen.
**pastoral poem:** Schäfergedicht, Idylle.
8 **tedious:** langweilig, ermüdend.
9 **clerical tasks:** Schreibarbeiten.
9 f. **Coleridge:** Samuel Taylor C. (1772–1834), englischer Dichter der Romantik.
14 **bless her yes:** mein Gott, ja.
18 **secretarial stuff:** Bürokram.

everything ready to be written, the first three chapters drafted indeed. And then she had to be looked into, of course, just in case. Another index card, another reference.

He got up. He beamed. He thanked. He took her warm, dry small hand and thanked again. He went out to the car, got in, looked back, waved, started the engine, glanced down at the AA road book open on the seat beside him.

And there she was suddenly at the car window, a little breathless, saying something he could not quite catch.

He switched the engine off.

"Letters?"

"Letters, Miss Rockingham?"

She hadn't known whether to mention, had wondered if it were perhaps better ... had thought suddenly, seeing him about to go, had decided that no, really, that it would be wrong, that ...

About two hundred letters, she thought. Upstairs. In two shoeboxes. No, three shoeboxes.

"Letters to whom, Miss Rockingham?"

To her. All of them. Two hundred.

They went back into the house. Upstairs. Into a spare bedroom with a whiff of damp to it and the sense of being for many years unslept in. And out of a cupboard came the boxes.

"If you would like to have a glance," she said, "to see if you might wish to make use of them. They are in chronological order."

8 **AA:** Abk. für *Automobile Association:* Automobilclub.
24 **whiff:** Hauch, Geruch.
29 **chronological:** chronologisch.

He took the first letter from the envelope. ". . . Until I saw you come into the room yesterday," wrote Lamprey, "I never understood the meaning of delight. I have never, until now, delighted. I have seen, since then, again and again, the door open and you walk in and my whole being has surged upwards. I cannot endure to wait until . . ."

He put the letter down and looked at her.

"Edward Lamprey and I," she said, a little stiffly, "loved each other for many years."

"Christ," said the girl. "How weird. I mean, how absolutely extraordinary. I bet you're thrilled."

"Hang on – I'll put another ten pence in. Hello? The thing is she won't let them out of the house which is fair enough but she's willing for me to make copies and thank God she's got an old typewriter so I can get going right away. She's extraordinarily helpful – set up a table for me and fussed round with electric fires and whatnot and now she's cooking us some sumptuous meal. Routed out some pyjamas, even."

"Oh," she said. "I see. So you won't . . ."

"No. Not this weekend. And I wanted to see you. I've been thinking about it all day. Hello?"

"Yes. I'm still here. Oh, well . . ."

"Thursday was – just incredible."

6 **to surge:** wogen, aufwallen.
11 **weird:** sonderbar, verrückt.
12 **thrilled:** begeistert, hingerissen.
18 f. **whatnot:** alles mögliche, was nicht alles, Dingsbums.
19 **sumptuous:** üppig, opulent.
20 **to rout out:** auftreiben.

"What?"

"I said Thursday was marvellous."

"Yes," she said. "Wasn't it. I've been thinking too ... Oh, bother. Never mind. How long do you think it'll take?"

"I don't know. They're long letters. Actually, they're beautiful. The most beautiful letters I've ever read. Love letters. They're – oh God I can't explain. It's going to change the book entirely, finding this. It's changed Lamprcy. I feel – oh, really involved for the first time. It's not just work any more, I actually care about him as a person. Oh, Christ, that's the last ten pence – look, I'll ring again tomorrow. O. K.?"

She stood in the doorway with a towel over one arm, and a pair of blue and white striped pyjamas. "I got these out for you, Malcolm. I think they would be about the right size."

Lamprey's?

"My brother," said Lucinda, "stayed here for several months before his death. Some of his things have not yet been cleared out." She looked in sudden doubt at the pyjamas. "But perhaps you would rather not. They have of course been laundered."

He held out his hand. "It's very kind of you. In fact the whole thing is extraordinarily kind. I can't tell you how grateful I am."

"It would be as well," she said, "to go to the chemist for the shaving things before they close. I thought we might take some sherry together at about seven, before

23 **to launder:** waschen (und bügeln).

we eat. There are one or two points I have thought of that may interest you."

There was sherry, good sherry at that, and whisky and gin and a soda siphon, magicked from heaven knows where in this surprising house. And Lucinda Rockingham wearing now some long velvet dressing-gown-like garment, looked pink and frail and yet, when it came to conversation, animated. And the Rayburn Maxistove had been lit and there was this extraordinarily good smell coming from the kitchen.

It was midnight before he went to bed. She had left him at eleven or so and he had sat on looking through the bundle of letters he would copy out the next day and, finally, reading some of Lamprey's poems. *The Cycle of the Year* sequence, written shortly after he met Lucinda Rockingham and which, knowing what one now knew, took on a new meaning. Overhead, boards delicately creaked, and presently there was silence. Outside, the occasional car rustled through the rain. He put the letters away, went to bed, lay awake for a while consumed with erotic yearnings, and fell asleep to dream of

3 **at that:** zudem, obendrein.
4 **soda siphon:** Siphon mit Sodawasser.
6 **velvet:** Samt.
**dressing-gown-like:** einem Morgenmantel ähnlich.
7 **frail:** zart, zerbrechlich, schwach.
8 **animated:** lebhaft, angeregt.
13 **bundle:** Bündel, Päckchen.
15 **sequence:** Sequenz, Folge, Serie.
17 **overhead:** oben, im Stockwerk darüber.
**board:** (Fußboden-)Diele.
18 **to creak:** knarren.
19 **to rustle:** rauschen.
21 **yearning:** Sehnsucht.

Lucinda Rockingham bicycling once, as she had described, along the waterfront with Edward Lamprey. A dog had run in front of his bike, causing him to fall and sprain an ankle. He had walked back to the house supported by Lucinda's arm. They had known one another, at that point, Lucinda thought, six weeks or so. Malcolm felt, in his dream, the touch of Lucinda's hand upon Lamprey's arm; he walked, with Lamprey, in a blaze of love.

"The amazing thing is," he said, "that they only saw each other at most every few months. Usually they met in London and every now and then he came down here. Her mother was alive then, and living with her so they weren't even alone that much if he came to the house. And then all the letters . . . Honestly, I wish I could . . . I'd love to read some of them to you. They're some of the best stuff he ever wrote."

"You certainly seem very involved in it all."

There was a pause.

"What are you doing?" he said. "At this minute. Apart from talking to me. So I can imagine."

"I'm looking out of the window. There's a white cat walking along the window ledge opposite. It's pouring with rain."

"It's chucking down here too. What are you wearing?"

4 **to sprain:** verstauchen.
9 **blaze:** loderndes Feuer, Flamme, Glanz.
23 **window ledge:** Fenstersims.
25 **to chuck:** hier: schütten, gießen.

"Oh, goodness," the girl said. "A sort of blue shirt thing. And jeans. How's it going – I mean apart from being good and all that – how much longer will it take?"

"Another week at least. I can't see any way of getting through before."

"Oh, gosh," she said.

He read and typed and the old lady brought him coffee and occasionally aspirin. Twice, they walked down to the sea, he with his hand hovering beside her arm across the roads. Edward Lamprey, she said, had loved to walk along the beach collecting driftwood. Yes, she said, the poem "Seashapes" was written after such a walk and yes, she supposed the references were more particular than might be supposed. She talked of a concert at the Maltings to which they had been together and of meetings in London, always with some shared activity in mind, visits to art galleries and places of interest and walks in Kew Gardens and Richmond Park. Lucinda Rockingham stayed with a cousin in Putney; Lamprey had a room in a friend's flat in Fulham which he used when in London. Each September they went to a Prom; in the spring they took the steamer to Greenwich.

7 **gosh:** Mann!, meine Güte!
10 **to hover:** schweben, verharren.
12 **driftwood:** Treibholz.
20 **Putney:** Stadtteil im Südwesten Londons.
21 **Fulham:** an Putney angrenzender Londoner Stadtteil.
23 **prom:** Promenadenkonzert (*the Proms:* seit 1895 in der Londoner Royal Albert Hall veranstaltete Sommerkonzerte).

And the letters, one upon another, a passionate narrative of love and commitment.

No, she said, we never travelled together. It would not have been possible. I had my mother to think of for many years; Edward took his family always to Cornwall. No, I never met his daughters; he talked of them a great deal, they were very close, I have a photograph of them when Marion was twelve and the others of course a little younger.

Year after year; through autumns and winters and springs and summers; moving from one longed-for, hoarded time to another.

She spoke of Lamprey's eclectic tastes, in music and in literature. She took down from the bookshelves the copies annotated in his hand, passages scored in the familiar red ink ("He used the same fountain pen for twelve years"), observations scribbled in the margins ("I have to confess that I never liked Edward's habit of defacing books, albeit with the best of intentions"). She peered into the intestines of the shining mahogany box in the corner, fiddled with slow crooked fingers,

12 **to hoard:** horten, aufsparen.
13 **eclectic:** eklektisch, auswählend.
15 **to annotate:** mit Anmerkungen versehen.
**to score:** markieren.
16 **fountain pen:** Füllfederhalter.
17 **to scribble:** kritzeln.
19 **to deface:** verunstalten.
**albeit:** obgleich, wenn auch.
20 **to peer:** gucken, spähen.
**intestines:** Eingeweide.
**mahogany:** Mahagoni.
21 **to fiddle:** fummeln, sich zu schaffen machen.
**crooked:** gekrümmt.

tutted and exclaimed, and produced, astonishingly, Duke Ellington and Sydney Bechet.

The rain turned to sunshine and the sunshine fell in wide mossy shafts upon the growing pile of letters on the deal table in the spare bedroom. Upon gaiety and sadness and delight and regret. Upon eighteen years.

"Soft lights and sweet music!" said the girl. "New Orleans and Eartha Kitt! Well, I never! What's a radiogram, by the way? I must say, if she wasn't eighty I'd feel I'd been cut out."

"My head's spinning. I've been at it six hours on the trot. I got so absorbed I didn't even hear her bring me in tea. It got cold. The cucumber sandwiches went soggy."

"All this vicarious experience. I don't know . . ."

"I had this dream about you last night."

"What was I doing?"

1 **to tut:** mißbilligende Laute äußern.
1 f. **Ellington / Bechet:** Duke E. (1899–1974) und Sydney B. (1897 bis 1959), amerikanische Jazz-Musiker.
4 **mossy:** moosig.
**shaft:** Strahl.
5 **deal table:** (Kiefern-)Holztisch.
**gaiety:** Fröhlichkeit.
8 **Kitt:** Eartha K. (geb. 1928), amerikanische Sängerin.
**Well, I never!:** Das ist ja unerhört!, unglaublich!
8 f. **radiogram:** Musiktruhe.
10 **to cut out:** ausstechen, verdrängen.
11 f. **on the trot:** am Stück, hintereinander.
12 **absorbed:** vertieft, absorbiert.
13 **cucumber:** Gurke.
14 **soggy:** matschig, durchweicht.
15 **vicarious:** stellvertretend, nachempfunden.

"I couldn't possibly tell you. It was disgraceful."

"Now, now," she said. Winds sighed and whistled across four counties.

"What?"

"I didn't say anything."

"It's ten days," he said, "since Thursday. Ten days and – six and a half hours."

"Look," said the girl, "I *know.* Don't I know."

"When I see you, I'm just going to . . ."

"I can't hear."

"It doesn't matter. At least it does. Darling."

"Listen," she said. "Have a break for a day or two. Come to London. You could always go straight back."

"No," he said. "No, I can't. I want to – goodness, I want to – but I can't. I'm right in the middle of it. You see there's something I just can't . . . There's an enormous thing I simply don't . . . Hello? Are you there?"

Miss Rockingham, in the interests of literary history I have to ask you if your relationship with the poet was a physical one?

Miss Rockingham, did you sleep with the man or did you not?

Perhaps, he told himself, it doesn't matter. So far as the book is concerned, it need never be stated. Prurience, after all, is only an arm's length away. The letters matter; the relationship matters; let the rest be silence.

But I need to know. For myself, not for the book. Be-

1 **disgraceful:** schändlich.
25 **prurience:** Lüsternheit, sexuelle Sensationsgier.

cause. Because I have read the letters and humbly experienced through them the feelings of Edward Lamprey and seen with the eyes of Edward Lamprey the woman he loved. Because I care.

They sat up late, with the radiogram turned low, and Lucinda Rockingham opened a bottle of madeira, a relic of her brother. She poured the madeira into crystal glasses off which the lamplight snapped, and talked of the onset of Lamprey's illness, of an afternoon in London when she had, for the first time, understood that he was dying. An exhibition at the Tate, she said. She turned the glass in her fingers and light flew from it into the corners of the room. Chagall, I remember, and Kandinsky.

"It seems a bit creepy to me," said the girl.

"You see I honestly do not know. I think it's quite possible they didn't. Which makes it all the more remarkable. The letters. All of it."

"I don't mean them. I mean you."

"Sorry?"

"You seem," she said resentfully, "to find them more compelling than real life."

He delved frantically in his pocket; the coin clunked.

7 **relic:** Relikt, Überbleibsel.
8 **to snap:** hier: blitzen, reflektieren.
9 **onset:** Beginn, Ausbruch.
11 **Tate:** *Tate Gallery:* Kunstmuseum in London.
15 **creepy:** unheimlich, abstoßend.
22 **compelling:** unwiderstehlich.
23 **to delve:** graben, suchen.
**frantically** (adv.): verzweifelt, hektisch.
**to clunk:** klacken.

"Hello? It's O. K., I've put another one in ... You sound cross. Please don't sound cross."

"I'm not," she said, "cross."

"Actually, I love you. What? I said, I *love* you."

"Oh ...," she said at last. "Oh, Malcolm."

"And I keep thinking ..."

"Yes?"

"Oh, just ... I keep thinking about us."

"You keep thinking," the girl said, "that we haven't been to bed together either?"

The pile of letters diminished. Lucinda Rockingham, standing at his elbow with a proffered cup of coffee said, "Dear me, I shall soon be losing you. One more day? Two more days?"

"Three, I think. Saturday should finish it. I'm never going to be able to thank you enough for all this."

"It has been a pleasure," she said graciously. "I've enjoyed your company. I lead a solitary life these days. It has done me good to talk. I hope I have not talked too much."

"Oh, goodness ... I don't know quite honestly when I've been more fascinated. You've – well, you've just changed everything for me, so far as the book is concerned. I only hope you will be happy with it, eventually. That you won't um ..."

"Have any regrets?" said Miss Rockingham. "I think not. I've thought it all over and am certain I made the

12 **to proffer:** anbieten.
17 **graciously** (adv.): huldvoll, freundlich, gütig.
18 **solitary:** einsam.
22 **fascinated:** fasziniert.

right decision. It is what Edward would have wished. Now that his wife is no longer alive. So – Saturday will be our last evening together."

"Thank goodness you rang. I was so terrified you might not. Listen, the most incredible thing. You know that friend of mine – the girl who plays in an orchestra at Snape? Well, she's driving down on Saturday and she said why not come along? Several of them have got this cottage and there's a room I could have for the night."

"That's amazing," he said. "That's wonderful."

"So what do you think? Shall I . . ."

"Is this room a big room?"

"Actually," she said, "I think it is quite a big room."

There were seventeen letters left. He read them through, in order, one after another, until the last. The final three were written from the nursing home in which Lamprey died.

There was no indication. Nothing to confirm, one way or another. Just as throughout.

"A cup of tea," said Lucinda Rockingham. "Earl Grey this morning. Edward had leanings towards Earl Grey. A small point I had forgotten to mention."

He pulled the typewriter towards him, smoothing out the one-hundred-and-seventy-sixth letter.

4 **to be terrified:** große Angst haben.
17 **nursing home:** Pflegeheim, Privatklinik.
21 **Earl Grey:** Teesorte.
22 **leaning:** Neigung, Vorliebe.

"We should hit Aldeburgh," the girl said, "at about six. So where shall we meet?"

"I'll ring you at this cottage place. Does it have a number?"

"Yes. Hang on. Here it is . . ."

"O. K. I've got that. Sixish? Wonderful. Twenty-four hours."

"I know. I can't believe it."

"I can't either. Yes, I can. I'm about ten years older, incidentally. Since the week before last."

"Silly . . ." she said. "How's it going, by the way?"

"Practically gone. All tied up, nearly."

"Have you found out if . . ."

"No." He looked through the glass of the phone box at grey sea marshalled beyond the sedate lamp-posts of the esplanade, at the back of a cast-iron bench, at the cold eye of a sea-gull. "No, I haven't."

"Does it still matter?"

"Yes," he said. "It does."

"Couldn't you ever so discreetly ask?"

"Christ, no."

"I have been thinking," said Lucinda Rockingham, "that in view of the fact that this is your last evening we might have a little celebration. I have ordered a duck

9 f. **incidentally** (adv.): übrigens, nebenbei bemerkt.
12 **tied up:** erledigt, unter Dach und Fach.
15 **to marshal:** anordnen, (an einen Platz) verweisen.
**sedate:** ruhig, gelassen.
16 **esplanade:** Esplanade, Strandpromenade.
**cast-iron:** gußeisern.
17 **sea-gull:** Möwe.

from the butcher and I find that happily there is a bottle of what seems to be quite a nice wine in the storeroom."

"Oh . . . Oh, that's terribly kind but in fact as it happens a friend of mine . . ."

"You were intending to stay overnight?"

"Well, I had been going to suggest actually that . . ."

"It has occurred to me that now you have read all the letters there may be one question that is bothering you."

He stared at her – neat, old, bent, her eyes bright amid a soft tissue of wrinkles. "Well – yes. Yes, there is – there is something I had been wondering about."

"This evening," said Miss Rockingham. "This evening over our little celebration, I think might be a suitable time."

"Oh," he said. "You've come. You're here. Did you have a good drive down?"

"I think so. I hardly noticed. Where are you?"

"In the phone box on the sea-front."

"Then you can drive over in about ten minutes. Look, I'll tell you how to get here, it's a turning off the coast road just after . . ."

A sea-gull gawped at him again, from the wall, with a metallic eye. "I tried to ring you in London. You'd gone. You see, the thing is she says . . ." The sea-gull raised its bill to the white sky and shouted; he could

11 **amid:** inmitten.
12 **wrinkle:** (Haut-)Falte.
24 **to gawp:** glotzen.
27 **bill:** Schnabel.

hardly hear his own words, his inexplicable inexcusable words ". . . so you see I must, I simply must. Shall I ring you say at eleven or so? She goes to bed then."

"I'm not sure," the girl said eventually. "That I'll be here. I may go over to Snape with Diana."

"Well, I'll try, shall I, all the same?"

"You can try," she said.

Miss Rockingham feared the duck was perhaps a little tough but thought the wine adequate. She allowed him to clear the table and moved with her still half-full glass into the sitting-room. She opened the front of the Rayburn Maxistove and stabbed energetically at the coals within. She sat down.

"You have presumably wondered about the nature of my relationship with Edward Lamprey. We were never lovers. In the physical sense."

"Oh," he said. "Yes. Quite. I see. Not that I . . . There would really be no reason to . . . For the purposes of the book."

"It was agreed between us. On account of his family. And now that that point is out of the way shall we have some music?"

Later, much later, when she was in bed, he walked down to the phone box. Youths with motorbikes revelled on the esplanade, spilling from the pubs; a small white dog trotted purposefully past the darkened shop

1 **inexplicable:** unerklärlich.
**inexcusable:** unentschuldbar.
12 **to stab:** stechen, stochern.
24 f. **to revel:** feiern, ausgelassen sein, sich vergnügen.
25 **to spill:** sich ergießen, strömen.

fronts; the sea slapped against a jetty. He dialled the girl's number. When it had rung a dozen times he put the receiver down and examined his feelings. He felt nothing, nothing at all. Just a faint regret, a pale decreasing sense of loss.

1 **to slap:** schlagen, klatschen.
**jetty:** Mole, Pier.

Fay Weldon

# The School Run

You know what it's like in the country. Too many roosters strutting round too many farmyards surrounded by adoring hens: too many bellowing bulls mounting too many grateful cows: too much soft-eyed female acquiescence and too much glittery male pride, too many females being chosen and males choosing to allow you to believe, as is possible in the city, that nature can be subdued and men and women made equal. The lesson from nature is too extreme to be ignored, and that, in my opinion, is why the villages hereabouts buzz with destructive scandal, and adultery, suicide, self-mutilation, incest, rape and murder are common occurrences, and cities are, by comparison, sane and peaceful places.

2 **school run:** Schulrunde, Fahrt zur Schule.
3 f. **rooster:** Hahn.
4 **to strut:** stolzieren.
5 **to adore:** anbeten, verehren, bewundern.
**to bellow:** brüllen.
6 f. **acquiescence:** Duldung, Ergebung, Fügsamkeit.
7 **glittery:** glänzend, funkelnd.
10 **to subdue:** unterwerfen, bezwingen.
12 **hereabouts:** hier in der Gegend.
**to buzz:** summen, schwirren.
13 **adultery:** Ehebruch.
13 f. **self-mutilation:** Selbstverstümmelung.
14 **incest:** Inzest.
15 **sane:** geistig gesund, normal.

My name is Judith. I come from the city. I am thirty-four. My husband is ill with asthma, which is why we moved down here. We have two children, Colleen and Kieron. We live opposite Ranstrock Farm, in a nice little old sub-Georgian house, rather cheap because it's near the main road. It's a rather new road, carving through the Ranstrock acres. We tend to live in a cloud of pesticide but never mind: the meadows are wonderfully green and lush and fertile. My husband makes architectural models – you know, those miniatures of new hospitals, new schools, new urban centres and so on, which serve to get commissions for architects and go on display to soothe the local inhabitants when it's obvious that change is neither wanted nor needed, but is going to happen.

(Round here I'm described as cynical and am not particularly welcome at the WI, because sometimes their cakes make me laugh. There is a certain Mrs. Leaf, who uses at least a teaspoon of green colouring and at least a teaspoon of orange colouring in her icing, not a drop or two like other people, and when I start laughing, so

5 **sub-Georgian:** teilweise aus der Zeit der Könige Georg I.–IV. (1714–1830).
6 f. **to carve through s.th.:** etwas zerschneiden, durchtrennen.
7 **acres:** Ländereien (acre: Flächenmaß; entspricht 4047 m$^2$).
8 **pesticide:** Pflanzenschutzmittel.
9 **lush:** saftig, üppig.
12 **commission:** Auftrag.
13 **to soothe:** beruhigen, besänftigen.
16 **cynical:** zynisch.
17 **WI:** Abk. für *Women's Institute*.
19 **colouring:** (Lebensmittel-)Farbe, Farbstoff.
20 **icing:** Zuckerguß.

does everyone else, which is half a relief, half terrifying, because once we start, when will we ever stop? Zen must come to Easter Dundon – our village – too, in the end. Nothing's safe. We all know it, but they'd prefer to put it off for a bit, not welcome it, like me. So I get labelled cynical.)

My husband is what you would describe as a craftsman, and I am what you would describe as a craftsman's wife.

Craftsmen's wives are on the whole good-looking, stable and reasonable. We wear well. Our husbands, after all, are not indifferent to appearance and have an eye for quality, and a weakness for a bit of gloss. They are practical men: they know they will never be rich but will always be *right*, and choose accordingly. They are often overtly gentle men, with anger and envy running in strong torrents beneath. But they love and are loved and are usually faithful. Their wives develop strong and fairly idiosyncratic views of their own, a kind of inner fortress within the outer defences of the craftsman's view of the world. Craftsmen tend to despise the world,

1 **terrifying:** erschreckend, furchtbar.
2 **Zen:** Zen-Buddhismus.
6 **to label:** etikettieren, abstempeln.
7 **craftsman:** Handwerker.
12 **indifferent:** gleichgültig.
13 **gloss:** (künstlicher) Glanz.
16 **overtly** (adv.): offenkundig.
17 **torrent:** reißender Strom, Sturzbach.
19 **idiosyncratic:** typisch, charakteristisch.
20 **fortress:** Festung.
**defences** (pl.): Verteidigungsanlage.
21 **to despise:** verachten.

because, being genuinely sensitive, they can't quite cope with it.

Artists' wives, if I may digress, have a far harder time. If your daughter must go to Art School, never let her do a Fine Art course. The young male artists are all waiting there to pounce, and pounce one will. Then watch her turn from some slim, bright, energetic girl into Saskia washing-up at Rembrandt's sink, soft, plump-armed, doe-eyed, bare-footed, serving the Artist who serves Art. Art is a convenient mistress for any man. He can drink, beat, steal, fornicate, commit any number of domestic cruelties and excesses in Her name. It's expected. And when your artist has sucked his Saskia dry and turned the corners of her smiling mouth from up to down, he throws her out and, if he can, finds another plumper, less currently weepy one. The process can take years, and a handful of children.

Want to sleep? Your artist wants to wake. Want to work – no – his retrospective's coming up. Want the baby? No – terminate! How can he paint if he can't sleep? *Don't* want a baby? Then you must have one – how can he live with the sterility you impose upon him?

1 f. **to cope with s.th.:** mit etwas zurechtkommen, fertig werden.
3 **to digress:** abschweifen.
6 **to pounce:** zuschlagen, sich (auf etwas) stürzen.
8 **Saskia:** S. van Uylenburgh, erste Frau Rembrandts.
9 **doe-eyed:** rehäugig.
11 **to fornicate:** Unzucht treiben.
16 **weepy:** weinerlich.
20 **retrospective:** Retrospektive, Rückschau.
23 **sterility:** Sterilität, Unfruchtbarkeit.

Want to eat? No, he wants to drink. And so must you, daughter, you must want what he wants, for you must serve Art too. But Art's a faithless mistress; pity the Artist: he only uses you as he is used. Serve Her as he may, drink, batter, carouse, fornicate at Her bidding, she'll turn her back in the end. Many, many are called, and few are chosen. Many have the symptoms of genius, but very few have the disease itself, and those that do probably look and behave like bank-clerks, and never even realized they were Artists.

(Bank-clerks as husbands are another story. I'll tell it some time.)

Farmers' wives – ah, farmers' wives. Sandra Jephsen lives across the way in Ranstrock Farm. At the Carnival Party last year Geoffrey Jephsen, cock of his dungheap, swaggering young farmer, Sandra's husband, owner of Ranstrock Farm and its three hundred acres, as was his father, his grandfather and his great-grandfather before him, let his eye light on me, and now I love him.

Sandra Jephsen has thin fair hair and a timid eye, fleshy legs and a gentle manner. A proper farmyard

3 **faithless:** untreu.
5 **to batter:** schlagen, mißhandeln.
**to carouse:** zechen.
14 f. **Carnival:** Karneval, Fasching.
15 f. **dungheap:** Misthaufen.
16 **swaggering:** stolzierend, wichtigtuerisch.
19 **to light:** fallen, sich niederlassen.
22 **fleshy:** fleischig, korpulent.

female, just right for Geoffrey, who glitters and glistens with male sweat and energy, and has muscles which move beneath the skin as if they had their own separate existence: as if it were they which made love, not he. I know that, I know all that; I don't care.

What does he see in her, when he could have me? I have long slim legs and sharp brown eyes and look and feel a bit like Shirley MacLaine.

He didn't want to marry her, he didn't choose her. He married her because she was a Fenton and the Fenton Farm's two hundred acres verge on to Ranstrock Farm, and that's the way things are done round here: a Jephsen and a Fenton sacrificed, so that two half-acre fields can become one one-acre field and the ploughing made easier. The old order continues alongside the new. They have two pale little children, more Fenton than Jephsen. I'm surprised she managed to impose her genes upon them at all, she has so little will, so little energy. She knows about me: I know she does. We take our cars out at the same time each morning – on the school run. Our children go to the same school, five miles down the road. She looks at me with her sad, pale eyes

1 **to glitter:** glänzen, funkeln.
**to glisten:** glänzen, glitzern.
8 **MacLaine:** Shirley MacL. (geb. 1934), amerikanische Filmschauspielerin.
11 **to verge on to s.th.:** an etwas grenzen.
15 **alongside:** neben, im gleichen Ausmaß.
17 **gene:** Gen, Erbfaktor.

and looks the other way and I know she knows, and I don't care.

I let her go first, I drive behind her, rather too close. I like her to know I'm there. I know it's cruel, but I don't care about that either. I see her eyes in the mirror, looking back at me if she has to stop and I pull up just behind her. My father was an artist, my mother killed herself (at any rate she died when I was twelve; that's how I interpret it. Suicide or second-hand murder). When *he* died last year there were two hundred canvases in the attic. He'd sold three when he was twenty-six, and nothing since. Nothing. Perhaps I inherit his cruelty? I burnt them all. I and my sister, we presided over the death of his life. It was a wonderful bonfire. Crackle crackle! My husband Roy was shocked. He doesn't like to see anything die that lives. He doesn't like to see Art, Craft's big sister, insulted. I think he changed his view of me a little, then. But how can I tell what's happening between him and me? It's all one-way now, in any case. I love Geoffrey. I've forgotten Roy. I would drive whey-faced Sandra off the road, if I dared, which I so nearly do. Except for the children, in the cars; for this is the school run.

Five miles to school there and back in the morning, and the same again in the afternoon. That's a hundred miles in a school week.

10 f. **canvas:** Leinwand; Gemälde auf Leinwand.
14 **bonfire:** (Freuden-)Feuer.
15 **to crackle:** knistern, prasseln.
21 **whey-faced:** käsig, käsebleich.

"It's crazy," says Roy. "Why don't you and Sandra Jephsen get together and organize something?"
"I like doing it," I say. She sometimes manages to elude me on the way home, but there I am in the morning, always, falling in just behind her. Well, the children do have to be at school on time. She's not a bad driver.

They closed our village school at the beginning of the year: it was either put the children on the school bus to Polydock Junior, which has a low reputation, or do the hundred weekly miles to Pennyham and back. How was I to know Sandra would choose Pennyham, too? I'm surprised she cares. I'm surprised she can tell a good school from a bad school. I can. I'm a real PTA type. Geoffrey says so.

Geoffrey said so, nuzzling my ear in the back of his Range Rover, my skirt rucked up and tearing, caught on the door handle, with the dogs snuffling and uneasy outside. It's quick, sudden, farmyard and violent with Geoffrey, not slow and gentle and peaceful and reverential as it is with Roy. Roy talks to me while he makes love, admires my body, looks after my feelings, goes on patiently till I'm satisfied: Geoffrey doesn't care

3 **to elude:** entgehen, ausweichen.
5 **to fall in:** sich anschließen.
13 **PTA:** Abk. für *Parent-Teacher Association:* Elternbeirat
15 **to nuzzle:** (mit dem Mund oder der Nase) liebkosen.
16 **to ruck up:** hochschieben, -rutschen.
17 **to snuffle:** schnüffeln, schnuppern.
**uneasy:** unruhig.
19 f. **reverential:** ehrfurchtsvoll, ehrerbietig.

about me, only about him. He loves me, in so far as he loves me, and while it lasts, for the sexual pleasure I give him. That's all. Geoffrey says things like, "what a little slut you are," or, "if I were your husband I'd throw you out," or, if I say I have to go, because of the children, "what a real little Miss PTA you are!" And then his teeth will nip my ear so I cry out and I don't go until he's finished, and the children wait at the school gate and I don't care. I love him. Sandra Jephsen collects hers on time, poor thing.

Why does he want her, standing in his kitchen, mashing the potatoes for his supper with her pale suffering eyes? He could have me.

I wonder if Roy knows. I don't care about that, either. He'd never have the courage to leave me. He loves me, he does what I say. He's weak. He's not strong. Geoffrey is strong, and so am I. Roy should have Sandra; I'm sure they'd suit each other.

Roy's asthma is worse down here in the country, not better. I used to feel for his wheezing and gasping – now I despise it. I'm never ill. He's half Geoffrey's size; he is really quite a small man, now I look at him. Is it really a man's job, to sit day after day gluing tiny scraps

4 **slut:** Schlampe, Luder, Nutte.
7 **to nip:** zwicken, kneifen.
11 **to mash:** stampfen, zu Brei quetschen.
20 **wheezing:** Keuchen, pfeifendes Atmen.
**gasping:** Keuchen, schweres Atmen, Atemnot.

of wood together? And not even to his own design, but to someone else's? He says that really he's a cabinet-maker, but he can't keep a family on that, so he has to do this. Compromise! I say I'd go out to work happily enough, even gratefully, but how would the children get to school? Roy doesn't drive. He has one of those peculiar disabilities which mean if you see a large object coming – like a truck – you drive into it, not away from it. A disability driving instructors fear, for there is no curing it. Or so Roy says. I wonder. I wonder about all kinds of things, since my father died, since I started this affair with Geoffrey. No, I didn't start it. Geoffrey did. We live in the country, after all, and the cock looks round the hens, and thinks, I'll have that one this morning, that pretty little feathered thing; and so he does.

We ought to move back to the city, where there's less pollen to fuel Roy's asthma, and I can get a job, and the children can catch buses. But I can't live without seeing Geoffrey. Not now. I would itch so much with desire I'd scratch myself to death and end up like my mother. Gone. When we part he says "see you round," but he never says how or where or when. He doesn't like me to be secure. I just know that somehow we see each other at least twice a week: I'm out looking for mushrooms or blackberries, or he just happens to be driving his Range Rover through Polydock when I'm shopping;

7 **disability:** Unfähigkeit, Unvermögen, Schwäche.
9 **driving instructor:** Fahrlehrer.
17 **pollen:** Pollen, Blütenstaub.
21 **see you round:** bis dann.

and once I knocked on his door when I knew she was out and he was in, because I can see everything from my window, and he had me on the bed, his and her bed, her side, and then said, "don't ever do that again", so I didn't. It's don't-ring-me-I'll-ring-you land we're living in. But he rings me. He does.

What do I do now, how do I get him, how do I make him leave her and take me? He can have me with or without the children. Roy can have those. My life can't go on with Roy for ever, humdrum and without passion. I shall never love anyone now but Geoffrey: the sheer power of my loving must make him love me: my hate for her will make her ill and make her old and die, and then he'll need someone to look after the children, and I'll be there. Roy doesn't need me: he's married to his architectural models.

Geoffrey took me to the tea-rooms at Pennyham today, for all the world to see.

"I'd love a cup of tea," he said, on the hay in the big barn, withdrawing himself from me, leaving me all a-shudder as usual with unfulfilled desire, but all the better to remember him by and all the more eager next time. "This is thirsty work," he said, and we went to the Golden Goose and had tea and scones; and there was a dark-haired girl serving who went quite pale and

10 **humdrum:** eintönig, langweilig.
12 **sheer:** schier, rein, pur.
21 **a-shudder:** bebend, erschauernd.
24 **scone:** Teegebäck, kleiner Kuchen.

shaky at the sight of him and me. You know how it is, you know: someone else's husband flirting with you, the wife's sitting opposite trying not to notice, you wait for the quick flicker of anxious eyes before deciding that's it, that's enough, and moving on. This was more than a quick flick and an anxious look; it was a white, open-mouthed stare, and I had no intention of moving on, not for Sandra, not for her, not for anyone.
"Who's that?" I asked.
"That's Ellen," he said, "that's last year's model. Don't worry."

I didn't worry. I took his hand to my mouth and held it there, for all the world to see. She fled to the kitchen. She was only a waitress; not worth a half of me. I didn't care who saw, and neither did he. All the world!

He ate his scone with big delicate fingers, big delicate fingers with which he paddled in me, and Sandra passed by outside and because we were sitting at the table by the window she saw us, and she came in and just stood by the table, in her headscarf, windcheater and clumsy leather boots. She reminded me of my mother. I have a photograph of her, standing just like

1 **shaky:** zittrig.
4 **flicker:** (Auf-)Flackern.
6 **flick:** schnelle, ruckartige Bewegung.
10 **model:** Model, Modell.
17 **to paddle:** (herum)tätscheln.
20 **headscarf:** Kopftuch.
**windcheater:** Windjacke.
21 **clumsy:** plump.

that on an autumn day, taken unawares. "What's the matter with you?" he said to her. "I can't be in here seeing Ellen, can I, because here I am having tea with Judith from across the way! You two really ought to get together some time over the school run. A hundred miles a week!"

She looked at me and I looked at her, and I smiled and she wept and ran from the room, and all the customers, the neighbours and the distant relatives, for that's what it's like in the country, turned and stared.

"Eat up," he said. "One thing in all the world I can't bear and that's a jealous woman."

I'm winning, I thought, I'm winning. She will die from grief and his displeasure, and I shall be queen in her place, as is only right and fitting.

It was time to collect the children from school, and when he'd quietly finished his tea he allowed me to go. My thighs were agreeably bruised and sore. He didn't make love to her, not any more. He'd said so. "Marriage is for the procreation of children," he'd said.

1 **to be taken unawares:** überrumpelt werden; heimlich geknipst werden.
14 **displeasure:** Mißfallen, Mißbilligung.
18 **thigh:** Schenkel.
**agreeably** (adv.): angenehm.
**bruised:** arg zugerichtet; mit blauen Flecken versehen.
**sore:** wund.
20 **procreation:** (Er-)Zeugung.

"And that's been seen to, after all. What you marry and what you fancy, they're two different things." He had a low, deep, soft voice. It caressed when it wanted to, bullied when it chose. What it said was what I believed.

I let her collect her children first from the school gate, and drive away. Then my Colleen and Kieron got in the back of my car. I don't let them in the front. It's safer in the back. I'm a nervous driver. My mother was killed in a car-crash, after all. She'd had a row with my father in the morning, and died in the afternoon. The whole house would shake with their rows. I was on her side, but hated her for not being happy all the same, and then I hated her for being dead, for making everything impossible: for example, that I could never make her happy. I promised the children ice-cream. I was alive and exultant; the sun was sinking. The autumn landscape was sodden and green and wonderful, multi-shadowed. There are lots of little hills round here, and sudden valleys and sudden views. Even when mad with love the beauty of it all impinges upon me.

I drove along the ridge-road, the A 561, not crowding Sandra at all. I could afford to be kind. He had claimed

3 **to caress:** liebkosen, zärtlich sein.
3 f. **to bully:** einschüchtern, kommandieren.
16 **exultant:** frohlockend, triumphierend.
17 **sodden:** durchweicht, vollgesogen, schwammig.
20 **to impinge upon s.o.:** jdn. beeindrucken, eine Wirkung auf jdn. haben.
21 **ridge-road:** Kammstraße.
**to crowd s.o.:** hier: jdn. bedrängen, dicht auf jdn. auffahren.
22 f. **to claim s.o.:** sich zu jdm. bekennen, jdn. anerkennen.

me in public, and disclaimed her. The A 561 was the main road between two small towns – not quite wide enough for the traffic it had to carry, always part closed for roadworks as they took out a curve here, or widened there, trying by half measures to make what was dangerous safe, and only half succeeding.

It was Carnival time: the time when floats from all over the West Country – which have taken their creators a year to devise, make and render mobile – gather in Bridgwater to begin their magical mystery tour of the West, and this road was one of the main routes along which these fantastical rolling monsters travelled. They would sometimes take up almost the entire width of the road, to the great handicap of the traffic and the great delight of Kieron and Colleen. As I rounded the sharp corner into the outskirts of Shillingford I found the road blocked. Before my eyes a petrol tanker was skewing and slipping one way across the road, a carnival float, an orange and green balsa wood and foam monster, fifty feet high, mounted on a long trailer, surrounded by pink polystyrene dwarves, and towed by a

4 **roadworks:** Straßen-, Bauarbeiten.
7 **float:** Karnevals-, Festwagen.
9 **mobile:** beweglich, fahrbar.
17 **petrol tanker:** Tankwagen.
18 **to skew:** schräg fahren, die Richtung verlieren.
19 **balsa wood:** Balsaholz (leichtes, großporiges Tropenholz).
20 **trailer:** Anhänger.
21 **polystyrene:** Polystyrol, Styropor.
**dwarf:** Zwerg.
**to tow:** (ab)schleppen, ziehen.

tractor, was skewing the other. The monster toppled on top of the tanker. The tractor tipped on its nose in someone's front garden; the tanker's cab tipped into the stone wall on the other side. The back of the tanker mounted the back of the trailer. The single car between me and this major traffic event jammed on its brakes. So did I. The car in front was Sandra's. I went into the back, but only slightly. Even so, my car being old and hers new, her crumple zone crumpled dramatically. My children squealed – I could see hers bobbing about in the back, presumably squealing too. I saw her eyes, pale and anxious with something other than wifely martyrdom, in the mirror. I saw men running away from the accident: the trailer driver somehow out of his cab, on to the wall, away. Fire! I thought, and I knew she thought it too. I restarted the engine, backed as fast as I could, which was very, very fast, and she followed. The children, catching fear, were suddenly dead silent. I gave her room to turn, then turned myself; a neat, rapid, three-point turn which any driving instructor would have admired, though in a place to turn him pale, on a blind corner.

But, listen, I looked after her and her children too. I was the opposite of murderous, when it came to it. We were both round the corner when the tanker went up

1 **to topple:** stürzen, kippen.
3 **cab:** Fahrerkabine.
9 **crumple zone:** Knautschzone.
10 **to squeal:** kreischen, quietschen, schreien.
**to bob:** sich ruckartig bewegen.
12 f. **martyrdom:** Märtyrertum.
22 **blind corner:** sichtbehindernde Kurve.

and the green and orange balsa and foam giant too, in a black stench of flame and fire, which – as I found out later – by some great good fortune killed no one. Fathers were not yet home from work: mothers were on the school run, or walking. Shillingford has the misfortune to be a fraction under three miles from both Pennyham and Polydock, which means the local authority won't pay for a school bus. (I'm sorry about these names, but if you live round here you have to put up with the truly unbelievable. If people who live in towns tend to believe the country has been invented for their benefit, it is hardly surprising.) Three houses were burned to the ground that day and new rules were laid down for carnivals floats and the movement of same that very week.

We took the long, difficult way round to Polydock, and home, over the levels. We didn't have to speak. She just smiled briefly, as I let her pass and go first. She knew the way home: I didn't. I followed behind, but meekly, not harassing. My hands were trembling on the wheel. Fear shakes you back into sanity.

I can't tell you how beautiful the evening was, or the little wet leafy roads, between the tall, tall hedges. If a hedge is high and the road runs low between them, you know the road is old, has been there for ever, or at any rate since people started wanting to get from one place

2 **stench:** Gestank.
10 **unbelievable:** unglaublich.
18 **meekly** (adv.): sanft, bescheiden, demütig.
19 **harassing:** belästigend, schikanierend.
20 **sanity:** geistige Gesundheit, Zurechnungsfähigkeit, Vernunft.

to another, and this was always the best and shortest way to do it. Even Kieron, seldom moved by natural glory, said, "doesn't it all look nice," and Colleen said, "don't say *anything*. We'll have a crash," and the last rays of sunlight glittered and caught in the gold leaves of the beech trees as they formed an arch above us, and Sandra's car went on ahead, showing the way.

As the sky darkened, the light from the blaze over in the east was pierced by orange and green streaks. It reminded me of Mrs. Leaf's funny cakes, the ones I shouldn't laugh at, and of my father's paintings, going up in smoke – he'd used a lot of green and orange, and painted very, very thickly, which meant very expensively, and my mother had complained about that, which I'd thought was unfair of her. A man had to paint what a man had to paint. If I'd gone harder into the back of Sandra's car, who would have been killed, her or me? Probably both of us. In my mind it had always been her, and I'd always been safe.

I knew it was all nonsense. Of course Geoffrey slept with her. (Why shouldn't he: she was there, and he wasn't so very fussy as to who he entered, or where, or how.) He had no intention of leaving her, was just acting rooster in the farmyard, and it was my fault for letting him; not his fault for doing it, or her fault for being

6 **beech tree:** Buche.
8 **blaze:** loderndes Feuer.
9 **to pierce:** durchbohren, -brechen, -dringen.
**streak:** Streifen, Strahl.
22 **fussy:** kleinlich, wählerisch.

hurt by it, if fault lay anywhere, which I doubted. I'd be last year's model too, soon enough, when my own marriage was sufficiently mangled to make him feel properly effective, properly seigneur of the lands round about. We were living in what had been the bailiff's home. No doubt his father had had it off with the bailiff's wife, and his father's father with her mother, and then they'd all stood round and watched the bull mounting the cows, and felt truly part of nature.

A pink flare leapt in the sky. One of the dwarves, I supposed. Even this far away, with the car windows closed, you could smell burning. Sandra switched on her headlights, and I switched on mine.

So I loved him, and that was partly animal, the good part, and partly full of hate, the bad part; and all mixed up with him preferring Sandra to me, and my mother's death and my father's paintings and the bonfire I had made, and shouldn't have, and I had hardly been sane since then.

All I could do now, by going on, was hurt her more. It was true that if it wasn't me it would be someone else. There were a dozen women thereabouts, bored and on the school run, who'd wrap their thighs round his, as

3 **mangled:** zerfetzt, kaputt.
4 **seigneur:** (Feudal-)Herr.
5 **bailiff:** Gutsverwalter.
6 **to have it off** (coll.): bumsen.
10 **flare:** aufflammender Lichtschein, Auflodern.
22 **thereabouts:** in der Nähe, im Umkreis.

excitedly, as desperately, as marvellously, as me. We all think we're something special, I daresay; men certainly do! It had just better not be me that did it. Let it be someone single, more purely victim. I loved him to hurt her, and it was demeaning to all of us.

She skidded on leaves and went into the ditch. I stopped. We all got out, and surveyed the damage. She said nothing. "I think it's a bit too hot for me to handle round here," I said. "We'll be selling the house very soon."

"Going back to the city?" She had a slightly nasal voice, and I had a flash of the old arrogant contempt, but another explosion, violet this time, brought me back to my senses. She was just ordinary. So was I. So was he. So were my parents – he and she, no different from many of our friends, only writ large on the canvas of a child's mind, by reason of her early death, and never properly reduced by time and experience and understanding to ordinary size.

"I should think so," I said. "All this driving about, just to get the children to school. It's different for you; you belong here."

"Don't sell the house without telling Geoffrey," she said. "I think he wants it back. It used to belong to the farm."

5 **demeaning:** erniedrigend, entwürdigend.
6 **to skid:** rutschen, schleudern.
11 **nasal:** nasal, näselnd.
16 **writ large:** im Großformat, übertrieben groß.
17 **by reason of:** wegen, infolge.

It occured to me, briefly, that if he'd been trying to get me out, this was the right way to go about it, but I don't really credit him with quite so much duplicity. Of course it might have been unconscious on his part. He came from noble baron stock, after all.

We didn't mention Geoffrey, apart from in the role of possible house-buyer. We didn't have to. She recognized an abdication when she heard one, and accepted it graciously. She had always been the rightful queen.

We pushed and levered her car back on to the road. She drove off, I followed. She went into her big house, I into my own lesser one. Roy looked up from a model of a new Canadian university he'd been working on for some months. He had trouble placing so many fir trees.

"So there you all are," he said. "I was worried. Some sort of accident on the road. There was a newsflash on local radio."

"Here we all are," I said. "Safe, sound, and back to normal." I made tea.

"I've been a bit mad since my father died," I said to him in bed that night.

3 **duplicity:** Falschheit, Doppelzüngigkeit.
5 **baron stock:** Baronsfamilie, Feudalherrengeschlecht.
8 **abdication:** Abdankung, Verzicht.
9 **graciously** (adv.): gnädig, huldvoll.
**rightful:** rechtmäßig.
10 **to lever:** stemmen.
14 f. **fir tree:** Tanne.
17 **newsflash:** Kurzmeldung.

"I know," he said. "Hell-bent on destruction."

"I think we'd better move back to the city," I said. "As soon as possible."

"Anything you say," he said, and an unkind person might have thought he was unduly passive, but I knew that he only waited for me to say what was in his mind, when I eventually came round to it, thus saving time, argument and energy.

1 **hell-bent:** versessen, wild.
5 **unduly** (adv.): unangemessen, unpassend, ungehörig.

Anne Enright

## Seascape

He stood like a young seminarian at the water's edge, refusing to see the bodies that were strewn all around him. His eyes rested on the cool line of the horizon, and sweat gathered in the white creases of his face. His only concessions to the sun were the jumper he had removed, which never left his hand, and the thick boots that stood waiting in the sand behind him. He seemed to be standing quite still, but in fact was edging his feet forward, inch by inch. After a while, a thin film of water pulled at his bare toes, and he leapt back. The jump was awkward, and when he turned to walk back up the beach, he had the loping, twisted stride of an old tramp. He belonged to the street, and not to the sea, because his eyes had that puzzled, childish look, and his mouth was hard.

A woman rose from the sea behind him, the water spilling from her shoulders and hair.

3 **seminarian:** Seminarist, Mitglied eines Priesterseminars.
4 **strewn:** verstreut.
6 **crease:** Falte.
7 **concession:** Zugeständnis.
**jumper:** Pullover.
14 **loping:** schwankend, ungleichmäßig.
**stride:** Schritt, Gang.
**tramp:** Vagabund, Landstreicher.
19 **to spill:** hier: tropfen, rinnen, spritzen.

"Daniel!" He stooped to pick up his boots, without turning around, so she ran up the slope after him, her body scattering a wet trail on the sand. The swimsuit she wore was azure blue, with a triangle of viridian at the neck, and her wet blonde hair had a greenish sheen in the strong light.

"Daniel," she said again, catching up with him, "are you coming in?"

"Nope." He still didn't turn around.

"You grunter! You pig!" She shook herself at him like a wet dog and he pulled away from the drops. When she was done, he caught her by the arms and pushed her into the sand, then laughed and walked on. There was a moment's shock before she screamed and scrabbled up again, then charged after him up the beach. The old boots banged together in his hand as he evaded her, but when he reached the towels he turned around and let himself be caught. She pushed him down and sat on his chest.

"You need the wash, you old pig. I should throw you in like a drowned cat."

1 **to stoop:** sich bücken.
3 **trail:** Spur, Pfad.
4 **azure blue:** azur-, himmelblau.
**triangle:** Dreieck.
**viridian:** chromgrün.
5 **sheen:** Glanz, Schimmer.
9 **nope** (coll.): nein.
10 **grunter:** Grunzer, Schwein.
11 **to pull away:** sich entfernen.
14 f. **to scrabble up:** sich aufrappeln.
16 **to bang:** schlagen, knallen.
**to evade:** ausweichen.

"I can't swim."

"You can't swim? Sure everyone can swim. I'll teach you."

"Of course I can swim."

"Liar." She swung off him.

"You are a liar," she said, picking up the towel, which was yellow like her hair. "You're always lying to me."

He lay on his back, his eyes slits in the glare of the sun. He seemed to be watching the sky. She flicked her body with the towel to get rid of the grit that had lodged in the creases, but he still didn't turn around. The laces of the boots were tangled in his hand and there were sweat marks and the marks of her wet body on his thick, old shirt.

"You like it," he said and rolled on his belly to watch her. She covered herself with the towel to block his gaze.

"And anyway . . . I don't," and he rolled back again with a small grunt.

He pursed his mouth. "Pour us a cup of tea, will you?" It was an old joke.

"Pour it yourself, you bad bastard. You're not in your mother's house now."

8 **slit:** Schlitz.
**glare:** greller Schein.
9 **to flick:** schlagen, schnippen.
10 **grit:** (grober) Sand, Sandkörner.
11 **lace:** Schnürsenkel.
12 **tangled:** verdreht, verheddert.
17 **gaze:** Blick, Starren.
19 **grunt:** Grunzen.
20 **to purse:** schürzen, zusammen-, verziehen.
22 **bastard:** Bastard, Mistkerl.

She sat there, for what seemed like a long time, and watched him sprawled damply on the sand. She did not stretch out, ignoring the freak weather with the confidence of one who already had the perfect tan. The colours of her swimsuit brightened in the sun.

After a while, she became aware of someone staring. It was a small child, naked as a cherub. He turned away from her when she looked up, and put his hands up to his face, but continued to watch her through his fingers.

"Hello." She smiled at him and he ducked away at the sound of her voice.

"Look," he said, suddenly bold, and with one hand still to his face, he pissed delicately on to the sand.

"Lovely," she said, at a loss – trying not to give the child a complex.

"No, it's not," he said, "it's very bold," and he ran off as his mother lumbered up after him; "Come back here and I'll give you a belt!"

"That's the woman for you," she told Daniel, as she caught the struggling child and trapped his legs in a pair of pants.

"A good, pink-skinned Irish ma with strap marks."

Daniel lay still.

2 **sprawled:** ausgebreitet, -gestreckt.
3 **freak:** außergewöhnlich, fantastisch.
4 **tan:** Sonnenbräune.
5 **to brighten:** heller werden, aufleuchten.
7 **cherub:** Cherub, Engel.
11 **to duck away:** sich ducken, den Kopf einziehen.
19 **to give s.o. a belt:** jdm. eine runterhauen.
23 **strap mark:** Trägerabdruck, -streifen.

"Strap marks and stretch marks and Dunne's nighties. A fine hoult for you in the bed at night." Daniel grunted assent.

"Well, take the old shirt off at least. You look like a maggot under a rock."

"I look," he said carefully, "like something the tide washed up."

Affairs, she thought, should stay in the place where they were conceived, they do not transplant well. He lay on the sand as though it were the gutter, while she turned her patch of towel into a little piece of the Riviera. Her face was drawn with effort.

"All I want," she finally said, with deliberation and a fake smoothness, "is an intelligent life. You *know* what I mean." He turned to face her and his eyes were both puzzled and wary.

"No, I don't," he said, and then as a small concession, "it was far from intelligence that I was reared."

1 **stretch mark:** Schwangerschaftsstreifen.
**Dunne:** *Dunne Stores* (pl.): irisches Kaufhaus.
**nightie** (coll.): Nachthemd.
2 **hoult** (dial.): *hold.*
3 **to grunt:** grunzen, brummen.
**assent:** Zustimmung.
5 **maggot:** Made, Larve.
9 **to conceive:** empfangen; ersinnen.
**to transplant:** verpflanzen.
10 **gutter:** Gosse.
12 **drawn:** verzerrt, angespannt.
13 **with deliberation:** mit Bedacht.
14 **fake:** falsch, vorgetäuscht, unecht.
16 **wary:** wachsam, argwöhnisch.
17 **concession:** Zugeständnis, Entgegenkommen.

"Well, start now," she said, "do my back." He lifted his head and looked along the beach.

"I will not."

"Pig."

She flicked out the towel then lay down on it, with her back to him. After a moment's pause he made his way across to her on his belly.

"Here," he said, taking the plastic bottle of sun oil from its dug-out in the sand. "What do I do with this?" He spilt some on his fingertips and slapped it on her back, then moved over the skin like a farmer with a new lamb.

"You're done," and quietly he lifted the hair from the nape of her neck. He stroked the side of her face, until her breathing eased, his eyes still out to sea.

"Did you see the body in the water?"

"Which one?" Her voice was muffled by her arms.

"With the clothes on."

"No."

"Floating on its face."

"No." Her voice had an edge to it.

"It was badly swelled. The gas brings them up, you know, after nine days."

"No, I did not see it."

"Pity." His hand left her face, and he lay down the length of her. After a while, he seemed to sleep.

9 **dug-out:** Höhle, Unterstand.
10 **to spill:** schütten, gießen.
**to slap:** klatschen.
14 **nape of the neck:** Nacken.
**to stroke:** streichen, streicheln.
17 **muffled:** gedämpft.

The afternoon wore on, and still neither of them moved. There was something obscene about the two forms lying so close together, one fully dressed and curved around the naked limbs of the other. She looked like a tropical fish in a dirty pond, with a bad old pike to protect her. Everyone around them was busy being amazed by the good weather, playing and shouting and soaking up the sun, but these two were not sunbathing or flirting. They were probably not even asleep.
The heat grew less intense, and as a slight breeze pulled at her hair, she stirred and slipped away from the curve of his body. She sat up and stared around her, as though surprised by what she saw, and then she reached for her bag and started to search around in it. She produced a bundle of postcards and a pen, and shuffled through them to find the right one. It was a picture of a cat in a window, reaching for the blind above her, with the sign "Guinness is good for you" posted on the wall outside.

Dear Fiona, (she wrote) the weather ist glorious. The lump is being lumpish, haven't seduced him into the sea as yet. Will you check the cat for me? Should

2 **obscene:** obszön, unanständig, anstößig.
6 **pike:** Hecht.
8 **to soak up:** aufsaugen.
11 **breeze:** Brise, leichter Wind.
16 **bundle:** Bündel, Päckchen.
**to shuffle through s.th.:** etwas durchblättern, schnell durchsehen.
19 **Guinness:** dunkles irisches Bier (Markenname).
22 **to seduce:** verführen.

> never have trusted her with that couple downstairs. We miss ickle pussums, we does, and you too.

She tore it up and took out a fresh one; this had a picture of a donkey and a red-headed girl with a turf creel in her arms.

> Dear Fiona, is he psychotic or what? The nights are, as always, amazing, but the weather doesn't seem to suit his sensitive skin. Besides, he keeps on sneaking downstairs to make dubious phone calls. I don't care about An Other Woman . . . maybe, but I keep fantasizing that he's got a kid salted away somewhere. If you see Timmy, say I'm fine, i. e. give him a crack in the gob and tell him I'm sorry. All is . . .

She had run out of space and was writing where the address should go. The breeze had brought up the hairs on her arms, and she paused for a moment to examine them. Then she started to write on the front of the card, over the donkey's face:

2 **ickle** (dial.): *little.*
**pussum** (dial.): *puss, pussy:* Mieze.
4 **turf:** Torf.
**creel:** (Weiden-)Korb.
6 **psychotic:** psychotisch, an einer Psychose leidend.
8 **to sneak:** (sich) schleichen.
9 **dubious:** zweifelhaft, fragwürdig.
10 f. **to fantasize:** sich vorstellen, fantasieren.
11 **to salt away:** einpökeln, sicher aufbewahren.
12 **crack:** (heftiger) Schlag.
13 **gob** (coll.): Schnauze.

I have lovely arms. Not that it makes any difference.

and she abandoned everything where it was and ran off down the strand, into the sea.

She could swim for hours. The water was beautiful, despite the cold, and she aimed straight for the horizon. She felt like diving down, wriggling out of the swimsuit and swimming on and on. The foolish picture of its limp blue and green washed up on the beach drifted into her mind. They might even accuse Daniel of the crime.

She took a breath, grabbed her knees to her chest and bobbed face down on the surface of the water. Slowly, as she ran out of breath, her muscles eased. She blew what was left in her lungs out in an explosion of bubbles, then shot up into the air and took breath. No. She would not be angry. Anger did not suit her. She would carry around instead the chic pain of an independent woman – the woman who did not whinge or demand, or get fat on children.

"I like independent women," he had said once.

"Bloody sure you do," she answered. "They're not allowed to complain."

The shadows had grown harsher and longer by the time she got out of the water, her hands numb and her legs

6 **to wriggle:** sich winden.
8 **limp:** schlaff.
**to drift:** treiben, getrieben werden, schwimmen.
12 **to bob:** sich auf und ab bewegen, wippen.
18 **to whinge** (dial.): winseln, jammern.
23 **harsh:** hart, scharf.
24 **numb:** starr, taub, empfindungslos.

stiff with the cold. She made her way up the slope heavily, shaking her fingers in front of her. Long before she reached their place, she saw that Daniel had gone. The postcard she had written and left was torn up like the first, the pieces scattered and half-buried in the sand. Among them was his discarded shirt, and a pair of trousers lay broken-limbed and empty on her yellow towel. She yanked at the towel to clear it of debris and the bundle of postcards flew up into the air. Moving slowly, and shivering with the cold she went to each one in turn and picked it up. Daniel had written on the face of them all.

The first was a picture of a Charollais cow on the cliffs of Moher. The sky was a hazy mauve, and the cow, which was right on the edge of the cliff, stared seductively at the viewer. Across the line of the sky he had written, "A Rathmines Madonna Dreams of The Intelligent Life." The next was a glossy reproduction of the beach in front of her, the colours artificially bright. Along the curve of the strand were the words, "Yes, the nights are amazing, but as yet, I have no child." She stared at it for a long time, and looked around to see

6 **discarded:** abgelegt (Kleidung).
8 **to yank:** ziehen, reißen.
**debris:** Überreste.
10 **to shiver:** zittern, frösteln.
13 **Charollais cow:** französische Rinderrasse.
13 f. **cliffs of Moher:** an der irischen Westküste gelegene Klippen.
14 **hazy:** verschwommen.
**mauve:** Malvenfarbe.
15 f. **seductively** (adv.): verführerisch.
17 **Rathmines:** Vorort von Dublin.
18 **glossy:** glänzend, Hochglanz-.

where Daniel could be, before picking up the next one. It had an oul fella sitting in a pub, the light bouncing off the polished surface of the bar counter and a fresh, new pint in the shaft of the sun. There was a crudely drawn balloon coming out of the old man's mouth with the words: "What *is* the difference between a pair of arms?" Finally, there was the beach again, though this time there were footprints drawn along the strand, enormously out of proportion, and a figure in the sea with HELP! coming from it. The caption read, "O Mary mo chree, I am afraid that the water will claim me back again."

"All washed up." The voice came from directly above her, and she gave a start. When she looked up he was there, perfectly dry. He was wearing a pair of navy high-waisted swimming trunks. His body was white as wax and his front was sticky with hair. She was ashamed to look at this body and so looked at his face.

"Oh all right," she said, and wanted to turn off the sun like a lamp, so they could make love on the beach.

2 **oul fella:** *old fellow.*
2 f. **to bounce off s.th.:** von etwas abprallen.
4 **shaft:** Strahl.
**crudely** (adv.): grob, kunstlos, ungelenk.
10 **caption:** Bildunterschrift.
10 f. **O Mary mo chree** (Ir.): *O Mary of my heart.*
15 **navy:** marineblau.

## Editorische Notiz

Das Glossar erklärt in der Regel alle Wörter, die nicht in *Reclams Englischem Wörterbuch* von Dieter Hamblock (Stuttgart: Reclam, 1996) verzeichnet sind. Die einzelnen Erzählungen sind unabhängig voneinander glossiert.

### *Im Glossar verwendete Abkürzungen*

| | |
|---|---|
| adv. | adverb |
| coll. | colloquial (umgangssprachlich) |
| dial. | dialectal (mundartlich) |
| Fr. | French |
| Ir. | Irish |
| o.s. | oneself |
| pl. | plural |
| prov. | proverbial (sprichwörtlich) |
| s.o. | someone |
| s.th. | something |
| vulg. | vulgar (vulgär, derb) |

# Textnachweise

Elizabeth Bowen: The Needlecase. In: E. B.: The Cat Jumps and Other Stories. London: Jonathan Cape, 1967 ([1]1934). S. 165–175. – Mit Genehmigung von Random House UK Limited, London, und The Estate of Elizabeth Bowen.

Anne Enright: Seascape. Erstdruck in: First Fictions. Introduction 10. 1989. Abdruck nach: David Marcus (Hrsg.): Irish Love Stories. London: Sceptre, 1994. S. 125–130. – Copyright © 1989 Anne Enright. Mit Genehmigung der Autorin.

D. H. Lawrence: Second Best. In: D. H. L.: The Complete Short Stories. Bd. 1. London: Heinemann, 1955. S. 212–220. – Mit Genehmigung von Laurence Pollinger Ltd., London, und The Estate of Frieda Lawrence Ravagli.

Doris Lessing: Flight. In: D. L.: The Habit of Loving. London: MacGibbon & Kee, 1966. S. 164–170. – Copyright © 1957 Doris Lessing. Mit Genehmigung von Jonathan Clowes Ltd., London, on behalf of Doris Lessing.

Penelope Lively: The Art of Biography. In: P. L.: Pack of Cards. Stories 1978–1986. Harmondsworth: Penguin, 1987. S. 219–227. – Copyright © 1978, 1980, 1981, 1982, 1984, 1985, 1986 Penelope Lively. Mit Genehmigung von David Higham Associates Ltd., London.

Katherine Mansfield: The Singing Lesson. In: K. M.: Collected Stories. London: Constable, 1948. S. 343–350.

Ian McEwan: First Loves, Last Rites. In: I. McE.: First Loves, Last Rites. London: Picador, 1976. S. 88–99. – Copyright © 1975 Ian McEwan. Mit Genehmigung der Paul & Peter Fritz AG, Zürich.

Frank O'Connor: Judas. In: F. O'C.: Short Stories. Bd. 2. London: Pan Books, 1990. S. 215–224. – Copyright © 1964 Frank O'Connor. Mit Genehmigung von The Peters Fraser and Dunlop Group Limited on behalf of The Estate of Frank O'Connor, London.

Fay Weldon: The School Run. In: F. W.: Polaris and Other Stories. London: Sceptre, 1994. S. 151–163. First published in 1985 by Hodder and Stoughton, London. – Copyright © 1984 Fay Weldon. Mit Genehmigung von Curtis Brown, London.

# Zu den Autoren und Stories

ELIZABETH BOWEN
7. 6. 1899 Dublin – 22. 2. 1973 London

Elizabeth Bowen entstammte einer angesehenen anglo-irischen Familie, deren Familiensitz Bowen's Court in der Grafschaft Cork auf eine Schenkung Cromwells zurückging. Private Schicksalsschläge wie eine schwere Erkrankung ihres Vaters und der frühe Tod ihrer Mutter sowie äußere Einwirkungen – der Erste Weltkrieg, der Osteraufstand in Irland und die Bürgerkriegswirren vor und nach der Gründung des Freistaates Irland – erschütterten das behütete Leben einer Tochter aus gutem Hause. Sie besuchte zwei Schulen in England und begann ein Kunststudium, widmete sich dann aber mehr dem Schreiben. Ihre erste Sammlung von Kurzgeschichten, *Encounters*, erschien 1923. Nach ihrer Eheschließung verbrachte sie einige Jahre in Oxford und zog dann nach London, wo sie als eine bedeutende Persönlichkeit des gesellschaftlichen und literarischen Lebens Freundschaften mit führenden Schriftstellern ihrer Zeit, u. a. mit Virginia Woolf, pflegte. In London erlebte sie auch den Zweiten Weltkrieg, eine Erfahrung, die den Hintergrund einiger ihrer besten Kurzgeschichten bildet. Neben einem umfangreichen Romanwerk und sechs Kurzgeschichtensammlungen veröffentlichte Elizabeth Bowen Essays und Rezensionen in Zeitschriften. Die hier abgedruckte Erzählung »The Needlecase« erschien erstmals in dem Band *The Cat Jumps and Other Stories* (London 1934).

Ausgewählte Sekundärliteratur: Allan E. Austin, *Elizabeth Bowen*, überarb. Aufl., Boston 1989; Phyllis Lassner, *Elizabeth Bowen: A Study of the Short Fiction*, New York 1991.

ANNE ENRIGHT
* 1962 Dublin

Anne Enright studierte am Trinity College in Dublin sowie an der University of East Anglia in Norwich. Für ihre erste Kurzgeschichtensammlung *The Portable Virgin* erhielt sie 1991 den Rooney Award for Irish Literature. 1995 erschien ihre zweite Buchveröffentlichung *The Wig My Father Wore.* Sie arbeitet als Produzentin und Regisseurin für den irischen Radio- und Fernsehsender Radio Telefis Eireann. Die vorliegende Erzählung »Seascape« erschien erstmals in *First Fictions: Introductions 10* (London 1989).

DAVID HERBERT LAWRENCE
11. 9. 1885 Eastwood – 2. 3. 1930 Vence (Frankreich)

Als Sohn eines Bergmannes wuchs D. H. Lawrence in beschränkten Verhältnissen auf und konnte keine seinen intellektuellen Neigungen entsprechende Schulbildung erhalten. Ein Stipendium ermöglichte ihm den Besuch des University College in Nottingham und die Ausbildung zum Lehrer. Er zog nach London und veröffentlichte erste Gedichte und Rezensionen sowie den Roman *The White Peacock* (1911). Seine Beziehung zu Frieda Weekly geb. von Richthofen brachte ihn ebenso in Konflikt mit der Gesellschaft wie seine Romane, die als unmoralisch empfunden wurden, da sie – wie auch viele seiner Kurzgeschichten – in ihrem Bestreben, die menschliche Natur und die geheimen Motivationen des Handelns unter der Oberfläche zu erforschen, psychologische, sexuelle und religiöse Aspekte thematisieren. Ausgedehnte Reisen nach Italien, Ceylon, Australien und Mexiko von 1919 bis zu seinem Tod entsprangen Lawrences Wunsch, Gesellschaftsformen und Lebensweisen kennenzulernen, die seiner Vorstellung vom eigentlichen Leben mehr entsprachen als die nordeuropäische Zivilisation, die er als lebensfeindlich empfand. Er fand einen Gegenentwurf dazu in der elementaren Lebens-kraft der Natur, in der Mythologie und in primitiven Kulturen. Neben Reiseberichten und Gedichten entstand in diesen Jahren eine Vielzahl von Kurzgeschichten. »Second Best« wurde erstmalig 1912 in der Zeitschrift *English Review* veröffentlicht und erschien dann in der Sammlung *The Prussian Officer and Other Stories* (London 1914).

Ausgewählte Sekundärliteratur: Michael Black, *D. H. Lawrence: The Early Fiction. A Commentary*, London 1986, S. 142 bis 146; Janice Hubbard Harris, *The Short Fiction of D. H. Lawrence*, New Brunswick 1984, S. 39 f.; Ernest W. Tedlock Jr., *D. H. Lawrence. Artist and Rebel. A Study of Lawrence's Fiction*, Albuquerque (New Mexico) 1963, S. 23 f.

DORIS LESSING
* 22. 10. 1919 Kermanshah (Persien)

Das Leben in britischen Kolonien prägte Doris May Lessing geb. Taylor und den Beginn ihrer schriftstellerischen Arbeit. 1924 zog sie mit ihren Eltern nach Rhodesien, wo sie die Schule besuchte und später als Sekretärin arbeitete. Nach zwei gescheiterten Ehen entschloß sie sich, 1949 nach England überzusiedeln, und veröffentlichte dort ihren ersten Roman *The Grass is Singing* (1950). Obgleich sie die Etikettierung als Schriftstellerin aus den Kolonien als zu einengend ablehnte, setzte sie sich bis Ende der fünfziger Jahre in ihren Werken vornehmlich mit ihren afrikanischen Erfahrungen auseinander. Ihr dritter Kurzgeschichtenband *The Habit of Loving* (1957) zeigt eine allmähliche Hinwendung zu britischen Schauplätzen. »Flight« geht zwar auf ein Erlebnis aus der Zeit in Afrika zurück, wurde aber in eine englische Umgebung versetzt. Trotz eines umfangreichen Romanwerks und vielfältiger Experimente mit anderen literarischen Formen betonte Doris Lessing immer wieder ihre Wertschätzung des Genres der Kurzgeschichte. Inhaltlich umfaßt ihr Werk ein breites Spektrum an Themen, das – mit unterschiedlichen Schwerpunkten in verschiedenen Lebensphasen – von politischem und gesellschaftlichem Engagement geprägt ist. Die vorliegende Erzählung »Flight« erschien in *The Habit of Loving* (London 1957).

Ausgewählte Sekundärliteratur: Dorothy Brewster, *Doris Lessing*, New York 1965, S. 80.

PENELOPE LIVELY
* 17. 3. 1933 Kairo

Penelope Lively verbrachte ihre Kindheit in Kairo, wo ihr Vater als Bankbeamter tätig war, und wurde nach dem Krieg als Zwölfjährige auf ein Internat in England geschickt. Anschließend studierte sie am St. Anne's College in Oxford Geschichte und arbeitete dort als Assistentin. Ihre schriftstellerische Arbeit begann mit Kinderbüchern, die bereits ihr zentrales Thema der Zeit und der Lebendigkeit der Vergangenheit in der Gegenwart erkennen lassen. 1977 erschien ihr erster Roman *The Road to Lichfield*, von den darauf folgenden wurden *Treasures of Time* (1979) und *Moon Tiger* (1987) mit dem National Book Award bzw. dem Booker Prize ausgezeichnet. Sie veröffentlichte eine größere Anzahl von Kurzgeschichten, wobei *Pack of Cards* (1986) die früheren Sammlungen *Nothing Missing but the Samovar* (1978) und *Corruption* (1984) mit einschließt, und arbeitet außerdem für Rundfunk und Fernsehen, unter anderem als Moderatorin in einer Sendung über Kinderliteratur. »The Art of Biography« erschien erstmals 1981 in der Zeitschrift *Good Housekeeping*, danach in *Corruption and Other Stories* (London 1984).

Ausgewählte Sekundärliteratur: Pierre Yvard, »*Pack of Cards*. A Theme and a Technique«, in: *Journal of the Short Story in English* 13 (1989) S. 103–111.

KATHERINE MANSFIELD (d. i. Kathleen Mansfield Beauchamp)
14. 10. 1888 Wellington (Neuseeland) – 17. 10. 1923 Fontainebleau (Frankreich)

Katherine Mansfield verbrachte ihre Kindheit in Neuseeland, wo sie bereits erste Geschichten für die Schulzeitung schrieb. Von 1903 bis 1906 besuchte sie zusammen mit ihren beiden Schwestern eine Schule in London und kehrte nur ungern nach Neuseeland zurück. Bereits 1908 kam sie wiederum nach London in der Hoffnung, zumindest einen Teil ihres Lebensunterhaltes als Schriftstellerin bestreiten zu können. Eine unerwünschte Schwangerschaft führte zu einer überstürzten Ehe und zur Flucht nach Bayern – Erlebnisse, die den Hintergrund zu ihrer ersten Kurzgeschichtensammlung *In a German Pension* (1911) bilden. Ihre Beziehung zu dem Schriftsteller und Literaturkritiker John Middleton Murry, den sie 1918 heiratete, gab ihrem Schreiben neue Impulse. Zwei weitere Sammlungen von Kurzgeschichten, *Bliss and Other Stories* (1920) und *The Garden Party and Other Stories* (1922), verarbeiten Erinnerungen an ihre Kindheit in Neuseeland. Sie gelten als wesentliche Marksteine in der Entwicklung der nachviktorianischen, modernen Kurzgeschichte englischer Sprache. 1915/1916 erkrankte Katherine Mansfield an Tuberkulose. Ihre letzten Lebensjahre verbrachte sie, auf Heilung hoffend, größtenteils in Südfrankreich. Die letzten beiden Sammlungen ihrer Kurzgeschichten, ihr Tagebuch und ihre Briefe wurden postum veröffentlicht. »The Singing Lesson« erschien in *The Garden Party and Other Stories* (New York / London 1922).

Ausgewählte Sekundärliteratur: Saralyn R. Daly, *Katherine Mansfield*, überarb. Neuaufl., New York 1994; Kate Fullbrook, *Katherine Mansfield*, Bloomington (Indiana) 1986.

IAN McEWAN
* 21. 6. 1948 Aldershot

Bedingt durch die militärische Laufbahn seines Vaters verbrachte Ian McEwan einen Teil seiner Kindheit an Stützpunkten wie Singapur und Libyen, bevor er in England ein Internat besuchte. Anschließend studierte er Literaturwissenschaft in Brighton und später in Norwich, wo er einen Magisterkurs im kreativen Schreiben bei Malcolm Bradbury belegte. Zwei der zum Examen eingereichten Kurzgeschichten übernahm er in seinen 1975 veröffentlichten Band *First Love, Last Rites*, für den er mit dem Somerset Maugham Award ausgezeichnet wurde. Ein wesentliches Merkmal seiner Geschichten sind die scheinbar trivialen Situationen, die eine schockierend-groteske Doppelbödigkeit offenbaren. Einem weiteren Kurzgeschichtenband folgte McEwans erster Roman *The Cement Garden* (1978). Neben weiteren Romanen umfaßt McEwans Werk Drehbücher für das Fernsehen sowie Feuilletonartikel. »First Love, Last Rites« erschien in dem gleichnamigen Band (London 1975).

Ausgewählte Sekundärliteratur: Ansgar Nünning, »Kurzgeschichten von Ian McEwan in einem Englischleistungskurs. Darstellung grotesker Welten aus der Perspektive des ›verrückten Monologisten‹«, in: *Literatur in Wissenschaft und Unterricht* 23 (1990) S. 36–50.

FRANK O'CONNOR (d. i. Michael Francis O'Donovan)
17. 9. 1903 Cork – 10. 3. 1966 Dublin

Als Sohn wenig begüterter Eltern konnte Frank O'Connor nur bis zu seinem fünfzehnten Lebensjahr die Schule besuchen. Seine frühesten schriftstellerischen Arbeiten – Gedichte und Essays – verfaßte er auf Gälisch. Sein zeitweiliges Engagement für die Irisch-Republikanische Armee führte zu einer Internierung des Zwanzigjährigen, anschließend arbeitete er als Bibliothekar in Sligo. Sein erster Kurzgeschichtenband *Guests of the Nation* erschien 1931 unter seinem Pseudonym. Von 1935 bis 1939 war O'Connor einer der Direktoren des berühmten Abbey Theatre in Dublin. Trotz seiner Beschäftigung mit dem Drama und weitgefächerter essayistischer und poetischer Arbeiten blieb die Kurzgeschichte die für ihn bedeutendste literarische Ausdrucksform. Von 1951 bis 1961 lehrte O'Connor an amerikanischen Universitäten. »Judas« erschien in einer frühen Fassung unter dem Titel »Night of the Stars« 1942. Die Geschichte wurde in ihrer späteren Form auch unter dem Titel »The Rivals« veröffentlicht.

Ausgewählte Sekundärliteratur: William M. Tomory, *Frank O'Connor*, Boston 1980, S. 124 ff.; Maurice Wohlgelernter, *Frank O'Connor. An Introduction*, New York 1977, S. 93 f.

## FAY WELDON

* 22. 9. 1931 Alvechurch (Worcestershire)

Mit dem Schreiben von Kurzgeschichten und Romanen setzte Fay Weldon eine Tradition ihrer Familie mütterlicherseits fort. Als einen weiteren prägenden Einfluß betrachtet sie selbst die Tatsache, daß sie nach der Scheidung ihrer Eltern und durch den Besuch einer Mädchenschule in einer von Frauen bestimmten Umwelt aufwuchs. Ihre frühe Kindheit verbrachte sie in Neuseeland, im Alter von vierzehn Jahren zog sie mit ihrer Mutter und Schwester nach London. Sie studierte Psychologie und Wirtschaftswissenschaften an der St. Andrew's University in Schottland. Neben einer erfolgreichen Karriere als Werbetexterin begann sie Drehbücher für das Fernsehen, Bühnenstücke und Hörspiele zu schreiben. Ihr erster Roman *The Fat Woman's Joke* (1967) entstand aus dem gleichnamigen Fernsehspiel. Romane wurden dann zum Schwerpunkt ihres Schreibens, dessen zentrales Thema Probleme und Bedürfnisse der Frau bilden. Fay Weldon veröffentlichte außerdem drei Sammlungen von Kurzgeschichten,

*Watching me, Watching you* (1981), *Polaris and Other Stories* (1985) und *Moon Over Minneapolis, or Why She Couldn't Stay* (1991). »The School Run« erschien in *Polaris and Other Stories* (London 1985).

Ausgewählte Sekundärliteratur: Ann Marie Hebert, »Rewriting the Feminine Script. Fay Weldon's Wicked Laughter«, in: *Critical Matrix* 7 (1993) S. 21–40; Olga Kenyon, *Women Novelists Today. A Survey of English Writing in the Seventies and Eighties*, Brighton 1988; Agate Nesaule Krouse, »Feminism and Art in Fay Weldon's Novels«, in: *Critique* 20 (1978), Heft 2, S. 5–20.

# Fremdsprachentexte

IN RECLAMS UNIVERSAL-BIBLIOTHEK

---

## Englische Prosa

Margaret Atwood: *Polarities.* Selected Stories. 170 S. UB 9008

James M. Barrie: *Peter Pan.* 219 S. UB 9294

John Buchan: *The Thirty-Nine Steps.* 221 S. UB 9051

Anthony Burgess: *A Clockwork Orange.* 261 S. UB 9281

Lewis Carroll: *Alice's Adventures in Wonderland.* Ill. 165 S. UB 9160

Gilbert Keith Chesterton: *Two Father Brown Stories.* 80 S. UB 9223

Joseph Conrad: *Heart of Darkness.* 189 S. UB 9161

Roald Dahl: *Three Tales of the Unexpected.* 96 S. UB 9215 – *The Witches.* 192 S. UB 9080

Charles Dickens: *A Christmas Carol.* 155 S. UB 9150

Arthur Conan Doyle: *The Speckled Band.* Four Sherlock Holmes Stories. 184 S. UB 9003

Daphne Du Maurier: *The Birds.* 76 S. UB 9287 – *Don't Look Now.* 109 S. UB 9054

*English Aphorisms.* 148 S. UB 9296

Nadine Gordimer: *Town and Country Lovers. Three Stories.* 96 S. UB 9237

Graham Greene: *The Basement Room.* Selected Stories. 144 S. UB 9015 – *The Third Man.* 173 S. UB 9180

James Herriot: *Yorkshire Tales.* 165 S. UB 9044

Aldous Huxley: *Brave New World.* 323 S. UB 9284

Christopher Isherwood: *Goodbye to Berlin.* 328 S. UB 9010

James Joyce: *Dubliners.* A Selection. 104 S. UB 9181

Judith Kerr: *When Hitler Stole Pink Rabbit.* 268 S. UB 9076

Rudyard Kipling: *The Jungle Book.* 219 S. UB 9244

John le Carré: *Call for the Dead.* 240 S. UB 9048

Doris Lessing: *Three African Stories.* 77 S. UB 9245 – *To Room Nineteen.* 72 S. UB 9151

Katherine Mansfield: *The Garden-Party.* Five Short Stories. 85 S. UB 9152

W. Somerset Maugham: *The Letter.* 75 S. UB 9183 – *Rain.* 88 S. UB 9061

Ian McEwan: *The Cement Garden.* 182 S. UB 9069

A. A. Milne: *Winnie-the-Pooh.* Ill. 180 S. UB 9231

George Orwell: *England Your England and Other Essays.* 122 S. UB 9024

Rosamunde Pilcher: *Snow in April.* 262 S. UB 9017

Salman Rushdie: *East, West.* 275 S. UB 9094

Alan Sillitoe: *The Loneliness of the Long-distance Runner.* 88 S. UB 9192 – *Saturday Night and Sunday Morning.* 360 S. UB 9038

Muriel Spark: *The Prime of Miss Jean Brodie.* 189 S. UB 9193

Robert Louis Stevenson: *The Bottle Imp.* 59 S. UB 9157 – *The Strange Case of Dr. Jekyll and Mr. Hyde.* 119 S. UB 9167 – *Treasure Island.* Ill. 334 S. UB 9258

J. R. R. Tolkien: *Farmer Giles of Ham.* Ill. 112 S. UB 9025

*Urban Legends.* 104 S. UB 9065

Evelyn Waugh: *The Loved One.* 192 S. UB 9233

Fay Weldon: *The Fat Woman's Joke.* 216 S. UB 9028

H. G. Wells: *The Invisible Man.* 270 S. UB 9013 – *The Time Machine.* 160 S. UB 9176

Oscar Wilde: *The Canterville Ghost.* 64 S. UB 9177 – *The Happy Prince and Other Tales.* 91 S. UB 9293 – *The Picture of Dorian Gray.* 344 S. UB 9019 – *Oscar Wilde for Pleasure.* 192 S. UB 9098

Virginia Woolf: *Mrs Dalloway's Party.* A Short Story Sequence. 93 S. UB 9196

---

Philipp Reclam jun. Stuttgart